CARTEL PUBLICATIONS
PRESENTS

PRETTY
KINGS II

Scarlett's Fever

T. STYLES

NATIONAL BEST SELLING AUTHOR OF *RAUNCHY*

ARE YOU ON OUR EMAIL LIST?

PUBLISHER'S NOTE:

This book is a work of fiction. Names, characters, businesses,
Organizations, places, events and incidents are the product of the
Author's imagination or are used fictionally. Any resemblance of
Actual persons, living or dead, events, or locales are entirely coincidental.

Library of Congress Control Number: 2013921262

ISBN 10: 0989084523

ISBN 13: 978-0989084529

Cover Design: Davida Baldwin www.oddballdsgn.com
Graphics: Davida Baldwin
www.thecartelpublications.com
First Edition

Printed in the United States of America

What's Up Fam,

Let me start by saying that this joint is one of our most highly anticipated sequels. BET called the first one a 'must read' and T. Styles has done an amazing job in the follow up to the original. "Pretty Kings 2" comes out the corner swinging and left me with my mouth open several times. It's so much drama and turmoil unfolding on each page that by the time you wrap your head around it all you're sadly at the end. I loved it and you will too!

Keeping in line with tradition, we want to give respect to a vet or trailblazer paving the way. With that said we would like to recognize:

Shonda Rhimes

Shonda Rhimes is a screenwriter, director and producer. She is best known as the head writer, creator and executive producer of the medical drama TV series, "Grey's Anatomy" and its spin off, "Private Practice". She is also the creator of the breakout political drama TV series, "Scandal". Ms. Rhimes continues to thrill audiences week after week with her creativity and we support her all the way. Make sure you check out her work, I promise, you will become addicted.

Ok, go 'head and dive in! I'll get at you in the next novel. Happy Holidays!

Be Easy!
Charisse "C. Wash" Washington
Vice President

The Cartel Publications
www.thecartelpublications.com
www.twitter.com/cartelbooks
www.facebook.com/cartelpublications
Follow us on Instagram: Cartelpublications

DEDICATION

This novel is dedicated to all my fans.

Twisted T. Styles

PROLOGUE

The moonlight from the open window shined against Scarlett Kennedy's pale white skin as she lie in the bed. She was suffering from a high fever. Although she was asleep her head shifted slowly from left to right, as she was held captive by her nightmare. She had done a lot of bad things over the past few months and now her mind kept her in prison, and forced her to relive each moment.

Race Kennedy, her sister-in-law, paced the floor in front of Scarlett's large cherry wood carved bed. The nine-millimeter in the back of her jeans rubbed against her flesh. She was worried about her because although they were only related by marriage, she loved her like she was her real sister.

Over the past six months, the Kennedy family had suffered great loss. There entire family was being torn apart member by member and Race was praying for a miracle.

Slowly Race approached Scarlett's bedside. She stood over her fever struck body and placed her hand on her arm. The heat rising from Scarlett's skin quickly warmed her hand.

"I don't know what's going on with you, Scarlett but I do know this; you can't die on me. You can't die on us. We've been through too much and if you leave me"— she paused— "if you leave us I don't think we'll ever be able to recover. You gotta fight. You gotta stay alive."

Race removed her hand and walked toward the window. She pushed the dark burgundy curtain further to the side and glanced into the darkness. The crickets sang softly in the background and a full moon lit up the night. It seemed eerie that although life inside the Kennedy compound was sorrowful, outside, under the purple sky, everything seemed peaceful.

Turning back around, Race leaned up against the wall and looked back down at Scarlett's body. The butt of her gun banged against her backbone. Suddenly she focused on the bedroom door.

"Bambi, I don't know what you planned but where are you? I need you to hurry up and get here now."

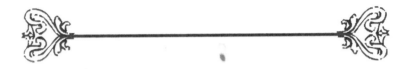

CHAPTER ONE
SCARLETT
6 MONTHS EARLIER

I scooped a pile of scrambled eggs and cheese onto the pink China plate and they knocked against the large sausage next to them. Carefully I walked over to the dining room table where Camp sat at the head. I nervously placed the plate in front of him, rubbed my pregnant belly and sat in the chair to his left.

"You said you wanted to talk earlier," I said softly. "I'm here."

I needed to choose my words carefully around Camp. I needed to do everything around him carefully. We were enemies in our own home and it killed me. I was always walking on eggshells.

Camp's dark eyes peered at me. I could feel the hate he had for me in his heart and I was afraid that nothing I did would make him feel better. And that included having his first child.

When he didn't speak I decided to fill the air between us with small talk. "I made your eggs the way you like them. With cheese and—"

Camp knocked the plate off the table, sending it spinning on the dining room floor. The fluffy yellow eggs popped on top of my foot and rested against my big toe.

I looked down at the mess that I spent twenty minutes cooking. Slowly I raised my head and looked into my husband's eyes. No matter how angry he was with me I loved him. More than I loved myself. It didn't hurt that he was so handsome with his smooth brown skin and boxer's physique. He spent a lot of time in the gym and his body reflected it. With all that said he resembled a monster at the moment. The monster that wanted my life.

"Camp, why do you hate me so much?" I asked softly. "Just because we aren't together doesn't mean we can't get along for the baby. Isn't that what you want? For us to have peace for our first child? Because without you I don't think I can do it. I need you by my side but I don't want us to be fighting and saying hurtful things to each other."

I looked into his eyes hoping I was talking some sense into him. But I couldn't read his expression. It was stone.

When he finally spoke his words sent chills down my spine.

"You just couldn't wait before you gave your pussy to another nigga?"

"I thought you were gone, Camp. I thought you were out of my life and I was lonely. And you told me you wanted a divorce before you left so I had nothing to hold onto even if you were alive. Don't you realize how much I love you? If there were the slightest chance that you still wanted me I wouldn't be in this situation now. Ngozi wouldn't be a factor."

"You don't get it," he said as he clenched his fists and knocked against the table with his knuckles. "It ain't 'bout you fucking somebody. I told you I wanted a divorce and that you could do what you wanted with your pussy. But you pregnant with my kid right now. Don't you have any respect for that shit? You due any day now, Scarlett. Yet you running around here letting other niggas dump inside your body on top of my seed."

Tears poured down my face and I wiped them away. Camp was stabbing at my heart repeatedly and he didn't care.

When Camp showed up that day with Kevin, Ramirez and Bradley outside of this house, and popped out of that white van, I thought I was dreaming. How could he be alive? I thought he was dead. My sisters-in-law and I all did.

It turned out that when the mass murderer came into the casino, the Kennedy Kings thought The Russians were trying to attack them by masquerading behind the killer. So while the bodies were dropping they were able escape as the killer went toward the back to murder more people.

Instead of telling us where they were, and that they were alive, they went into hiding. They said the reason they stayed away was because they hoped that The Russians would believe that they were actually dead. When someone who they won't say, let them know that things were going well and that we were making money, they believed the coast was clear and returned to us. I don't know about my sisters but it never sat right with me how they treated us.

I brought my suspicions to the other sisters and only one agreed that something else was up with them. It was Bambi. Her and I felt the same way. That they didn't trust us and that they felt *we* had something to do with the hit at the casino. Why else would they not tell us they were okay? We were married to them. If they can't trust us whom can they trust?

"Camp, this is so unfair to me. All I ever wanted was to love you."

"Oh that's how you remember it?"

"I had my problems but all marriages have troubles. Why didn't you want to stay with me?"

"Because of your temper. I can't have no woman hitting me in my face every time she get mad or shit don't go her way. Before you I never been with somebody so violent. You had me wanting to hurt you, Scarlett. Real bad. And that ain't my makeup."

He was right. Sometimes I was overwhelmed with anger and I didn't know how to deal with it. When I was able to control it a little I would scratch his car or rip up his clothes. But when you have as much money as he does, none of that fazed him. He just simply bought more clothes. Nothing seemed to bother him so I...sometimes I...hit him.

"I understand that we couldn't work because of my temper."

"So what you talking about then?"

"I'm just trying to get you to understand why I moved on. If you didn't want me when you were alive there was nothing I could hold onto after I thought you were dead. I'm not like you, Camp. I get lonely and I needed somebody to—"

"Take care of you," he said interrupting me.

"That's not fair!"

"It may not be fair but it's true."

He moved around in the seat and clenched his fists.

"Camp, if you don't want me to be with him I—"

"Naw, you can do you." He gritted his teeth. "Because even if you left that nigga it don't mean I'ma take you back." He knocked loudly on the table again. "I should've listened to my aunt Bunny though. I ain't have no business fucking no white bitch."

The air felt like it was knocked out of my body. "Why is it that every time we get into it you strike me hard by bringing up my race?" I asked raising my voice. "I already know I'm white. I was white when you met me. I was white when you married me. I was white when you left me and I'm the white woman carrying *our* black baby. I deserve more respect than that!"

I paused and looked over at him. I wanted to detect one ounce of remorse. I didn't see anything and that made me hate him.

"Don't remind me, Scarlett. I chose badly and it's the one mistake I wish I could take back."

Warm tears ran down my face. "You're so hateful!"

"And you a whore."

"Camp!"

"You are," he yelled back. "If you continue to let that nigga stick his dick in you while you housing my baby that's the only thing I'ma call you. I'ma start treating you how you deserve to be treated. And then you got the nerve to be sleeping with this nigga carrying the Kennedy name. You a disgrace to my family."

"Do you still want me or not, Camp?" I asked skipping the subject. Sweat rolled down my forehead. "All you gotta do is say the word and it's done. I'll drop Ngozi with the quickness because that's what this marriage means to me. But you gotta tell me now because I'm lost."

His expression softened and I was hopeful that he would say he wanted to work on us. Instead he did what he always did lately— hurt my feelings.

"I guess I wasn't black enough for you huh?" he asked looking into my eyes. "You had to take it to the mother land and get a nigga straight from Africa. I hope you getting dicked down good though."

"You are so wrong." I wiped the tears from my face.

He punched his fist into the table, which caused the dishes on top of it to rattle. "No, what's wrong is me having to come home after being on the run and having to kick another nigga out my bed. It's one thing to do you, but then you had the nerve to bring dude inside of our house and our bed. If I was dead I'd be rolling over in my grave right now." He pulled his hands together and put them in his lap. "The more I think about it I realize that I should've never fucked with white bitches. Ya'll all the same. Greedy and self-centered."

All I could do was look at him. His perfectly bronzed skin. His thick eyebrows and his full lips. Since silence stood between us I glanced over his chin, and then down to his chest and his arms. When I was done I looked back into his eyes. It was as if I saw him for the first time because finally the truth smacked me in the face. He didn't love me anymore. The only thing he wanted to do was hurt me and make me pay. We truly were over and there was nothing else I could do. I know that now.

"I won't bother you anymore, Camp." I picked the food up off the floor and put it on the plate. I walked it over to the kitchen and placed it on the counter. "I'm done fighting for you."

"So now you wanna play the martyr?"

"It ain't about playing the martyr. It's about the fact that I now understand that you hate me. I also realize something else. We moved quickly when we got married. We didn't get a chance to know one another before we decided to share a life together. Big mistake on both of our parts. Add on top of that, that we're involved in an interracial relationship and things are just unbearable. But you need to know this, I love you and even when Ngozi's dick was inside of my body, I never stopped whispering your name. I never stopped thinking about you. It may be wrong but I'm not afraid to admit it."

There was a car beep outside and I knew who it was— Ngozi.

"You bought the nigga a car and everything huh?"

I shook my head. I was done arguing with Camp. If he truly wanted it over it would be just that. But it was time for me to hurt his feelings like he did mine.

"What I buy Ngozi and what I do to him ain't got shit to do with you. Remember? You don't want me."

"Be glad my mother raised me right, Scarlett."

"And why is that?"

"Because I would've smashed your skull in just now."

"What about the black baby I'm carrying?" I said sarcastically. "Since you don't care about my white ass you gotta remember that."

"At this point I wouldn't even give a fuck."

I walked toward the couch in the living room, grabbed my butter colored Hermes bag and looked back at him.

"If you don't give a fuck about this baby, there are always things I can do to correct the situation. Don't test me, Camp. Like I said you never got the chance to really know me. But I do know you and your weaknesses."

I eased into the passenger seat of Ngozi's cream BMW that I bought him when I thought Camp was dead. He handed me a beautiful long stemmed rose and grinned at me. I smiled back.

He was cute with his high cheekbones and dark chocolate skin. Although he looked in my opinion younger than me, he was actually about five years older.

I met Ngozi when I was at the lowest point of my life. Although I never dated black men before Camp, I was hoping to recreate the experience by dating Ngozi. I know it sounds ignorant on my part but it was the way I was thinking at the time. I missed Camp more than I realized back then and it messed my mind up. So I started dating. I didn't just date black men originally. I had been with some white men too, but for some reason I didn't feel the same. I can't explain it. I don't know if the taboo made me more attracted to black men or if I was trying to replace Camp. Whatever the reason when I met Ngozi I was really ready for change.

It was the weekend and I was out looking for baby furniture at CRIBS baby store in Washington DC. I was frustrated because the crib I specially ordered was not ready even though it was supposed to be. I was having words with the young cashier when Ngozi walked up behind me and exchanged African dialogue with her. The cashier didn't have an accent so I didn't know she was from another country. But there they were talking for a few minutes and for some reason I was intrigued. Although she was rude to me, she was all smiles and giggles with him.

After Ngozi finished with her the situation was handled. In the end she made a call to another furniture store that promised that the crib would be at my house in two days. Which was a far cry from the two weeks she told me when I first walked in.

I was about to leave out of the store until he gently grabbed my hand. "Is there anything else I can do for my future wife?" Ngozi asked me in a heavy accent as he leaned against the counter.

I smiled and took him in. Ngozi stood six feet two inches tall and had a smile to die for. I could tell based on what he wore that he dressed similarly to Camp, which meant he only wore the best. I started to walk out on him because he seemed too cocky but for whatever reason I didn't. Bambi tells me all the time that boredom is the devil. Maybe that's my problem.

"You're really presumptuous aren't you?" I eased my hand out of his. "To touch a woman who doesn't belong to you?"

"It's not called presumption in my book, queen. I just know what I want and waste no time with games." He softly held my hand again and I didn't snatch away.

"I hear you but there's one problem," I said.

"And what's that?"

"I can't be your wife."

"And why is that?"

"Because I'm married."

"You're not married," he said playfully. "Maybe on paper but not in life."

I frowned. "What makes you think that?"

"I can tell by the way you're smiling at me. If you belonged to another man it wouldn't be so easy to captivate your attention." He was right.

He took a thick strand of my red hair and pulled it behind my ear.

After that day wherever I went he went with me. Before long I found out he was broke but it didn't matter to me. With the way things were going I had more money than I could spend. Bambi said that was the reason he latched onto me but I didn't believe her. I knew he was falling in love with me and I wanted so hard to love him back.

Not to mention the fact that sex with Ngozi was amazing. It only took a couple of months before we started acting like a couple. We fought hard but fucked harder. When I was feeling depressed, or thinking about Camp, he would kiss my tears away and fuck me until I felt better. He used sex to answer all of my questions and I was blinded by lust but I liked it that way.

Before long I moved him into my house, bought him a BMW, and called him my man. Although Denim and Race made it known that they didn't think he was good for me, Bambi was different. At first the only thing Bambi did was give me two thumbs down. She didn't start speaking her mind until he started asking for money.

"How's my Snow Bunny doing?" Ngozi asked me as we pulled away from the house.

"Not good," I admitted still thinking about my fight with Camp.

He looked over at me like he really cared about me. "What's going on? That nigga bothering you again? Because you belong to me now and I won't have him treating you badly."

"It's nothing like that," I lied.

"Then what is it?"

I smiled at him again. "All I want to do is hang out with you and have a good time. Okay?"

"Cool," he winked.

He drove down the street in silence. Five minutes passed before he said, "How much longer are you going to live in that house? I'm a man, Scarlett. And I can't stand by and watch what he does to you."

"He's still my husband."

He sighed loudly. "Why do you keep telling me that? Don't you think I know you are married to him? How do you think that makes me feel?"

I looked over at his angry face. "I'm sorry, Ngozi. I just want to be real with you that's all."

"Be honest, you're with him for the money right?"

"No, I'm with him because...well...we are having a baby."

"It's the money. If I had enough money to buy a home then maybe you could stay with me. I'm such a loser."

I touched is leg. "Ngozi, don't come down on yourself. You don't need a house to be with me. I'm okay spending time with you in the apartment."

"But I'm not. I want a home, Scarlett. A place where I can take care of you."

I removed my hand and leaned back into my seat. I crossed my arms over my chest and they rested on my large belly. "So you want some more money?"

He slowly pulled the car over. He parked and stared at me. "I don't want your money, Scarlett." He rubbed my cheek with his cold hand. "I know Bambi and the rest of them chicks put those things into your head. That's just because they hate to see a black man with a white woman. Don't you see what's happening?"

"I don't think that's the reason," I responded very annoyed.

"You wouldn't see it that way because you are a very nice person. But I know women like Bambi and the rest of them. They hate what we have. Don't let them stand in our way." He turned my chin toward him and kissed my lips. "Don't let anybody come in the way of us. Okay?"

I smiled. That's one thing about Ngozi that I loved. He might not be Camp but he is an excellent stand in.

When our kiss was over he pulled back into traffic. I looked over at him and smiled. I don't love him but I care about him a lot. Maybe things can work out for us after all.

"Scarlett, I don't want your money but I do want you to give some thought to the house. It's like you tell me all of the time, it's not like you don't have the money right? You might as well give it to somebody you love."

"I'll see about transferring some money later this week," I said feeling betrayed.

He grinned widely. "That's my baby."

CHAPTER TWO
RACE

I was in the shower with the warm water falling over my head. When I heard Scarlett and Camp fighting earlier. I was almost blown and unable to enjoy my morning. I guess the dude Ngozi is causing major problems in their marriage. I feel bad for my sister. But unlike their crazy situation, at the moment anyway, I was living the life of my dreams.

The pink Caress soap and the washcloth were clasped tightly in my hand as I held it under the water. I was in heaven until I felt a small kiss on the back of my shoulder. When I turned around I was looking into Carey's beautiful brown eyes. I winked at her before kissing her soft pink lips. She eased the soap and washcloth out of my hand and threw them to the bathtub's floor. They made a small thud sound. I turned around and faced her.

"What you need that for?" she asked me. "I'm about to lick you clean."

She pushed me up against the wall. My back pressed against the warm porcelain tiles. She dropped to her knees and threw my left leg over her shoulder. She parted my pussy lips and her warm tongue circled my clit. I bit down on my bottom lip and moaned. I was feeling like a rock star.

While she licked my pussy clean Ramirez, my husband, walked up to me. He placed his hand behind my neck and eased his tongue between my lips and into my mouth. His chest pressed against my breasts and it seemed like every part of my body trembled.

The three of us had been fucking nonstop since he came back from the dead and life was perfect. After all, I got the best of both worlds. Mostly every night I sleep with the man I love and the woman of my dreams. Who could ask for more? When you think about it I had it made. I could sleep with Carey and my husband every night in the same bed and we all cared about each other. In the heat of the moment it felt something like love.

When Ramirez first returned home after being gone so long, I thought it would be a problem when he knew that Carey and I had continued on our relationship without him. I felt real bad because her and I didn't skip a beat. Not only were Carey and I an item, I put her up in a beautiful house and bought her two cars. I wanted her to know that although I wasn't Ramirez, I could still take care of her. She deserved the money too.

She did all she could to make me feel wanted and special. If I was hungry she cooked. If my bedroom was dirty she cleaned up behind me. She nurtured my need to be loved and wanted and I was stronger with her in my life even though I thought I lost Ramirez forever. So when he came back I assumed things would be weird. Instead he embraced us both and suddenly my life seemed complete. I had the man and the girl.

When me, Carey and Ramirez had an understanding about our relationship, I came out to my sisters and told them I enjoyed women. Denim and Scarlett was all for my happiness but Bambi was having none of it. She called it an abomination and promised I would be going to hell. But I reminded her about all of the people she killed. She got angry and told me to kill myself instead. I guess she was just that mad.

It didn't take me long to realize that our situation didn't require validation from people not sharing our bedroom. So we moved on and did what we did best.

Since Ramirez was okay with Carey being in the house, last week we told Carey that we want her here Monday through Friday. That didn't go over well at all. Because Bambi made it her business, every time she saw Carey, to call her a bitch.

I love Bambi but she gotta realize that this is my life. And although my marriage might not be the epitome of what she envisioned for herself or me, it works for the three of us. Every night when I go to sleep, to the right I had my husband, and to the left was Carey. Shit was sweet. Who wouldn't want a scenario like this every night?

After Carey licked me until I shivered and came all on her plush lips, Ramirez bent me over on the wall and fucked me until my pussy lips were raw. He wanted me to know that he was in charge.

It's funny. When I was out in the streets I controlled the Pretty Kings Empire under Bambi's rule. But when I came home I was all his and to tell you the truth I don't know how I felt about it. I had to be a little submissive.

Sometimes I felt like Carey and Ramirez were fighting for position when it came to my heart and sex. Whenever we fucked they tried to outdo the other and make me scream the loudest. If you ask me I can't say who is the best. But I do know this, since I started having them both my voice got deeper due to me staying hoarse all the time.

When we were done fooling around we dried each other off and walked out the bedroom. Carey switched toward the suitcase on the floor to grab something to wear and Ramirez went to the closet. I went to my dresser and grabbed a pair of True Religion blue jeans and a black t-shirt. I smoothed some coconut oil over my skin and looked at Carey and Ramirez getting dressed through the mirror. All I could do was smile. Wow! This was actually my life!

When my cell phone rang, the one that let me know there was danger, I picked it up answered it. "What's up?" I pressed the phone against my ear and it rested on my shoulder.

"Hey, Race. It's me, Sarge."

Although I was in charge of muscle for the Pretty King Empire, Sarge taught me everything I knew about guns and how to pull a trigger accurately. He was precise with his lessons too. He made sure I knew how to clean and load a weapon and how to hit my target every time.

He taught me how to act before my opponent especially when a clear answer wasn't present, to throw my enemy off guard. He was in the army with Bambi when she was in the service, and although I didn't fuck with him at first, he was now invaluable to our organization and me. More than anything he had become one of my closest friends and I trusted him with my life.

"What's wrong?"

"The Southeast Kittens are at it again." He sighed. "They just took out one of our soldier's eyes with a fireplace poker. I don't know what's going on with these girls but it's time to be swift."

"They don't like that Bambi gave some of their territory to the Pitbulls in A Skirt," I told him.

"So what you want to do? These young bitches are out of control."

"For starters tell Chucky I said to cut them off supply. They done in these streets. And I'm on my way now. Just give me a—"

"I got it, Race," Sarge said interrupting me. "I just wanted to give you an update before I made a move. The last time I went into action without your blessings you went ballistic on me." He laughed. "I'm a fast learner."

I smiled. Even though I wanted to get involved because I loved the drama of the streets, my husband and wifey did have plans for dinner later and I didn't want to ruin them by doing something that I didn't have to. Bambi always told me to delegate and maybe it was time.

"Aight, Sarge. Just get at me later and let me know what happened. If shit don't go your way tell me ASAP. I gotta know what's going on."

"Already on it."

When I hung up with him, Ramirez walked over to me, put his arms around my waist and whispered in my ear. "You know that shit turns me on right?"

"What shit?" I said putting on my earrings as he clung to me like a warm sweater.

"How you be laying the murder game down."

"You weird, Ramirez. What about that shit turns you on?"

"Everything and ain't nothing 'bout it weird. You gotta understand my point of view."

I giggled. "And what's that?"

"Before I left you were all quiet and shy and now you this beast who don't hesitate to push off. What isn't there to love about that shit? I'm proud of you, ma. You stepped up when the time came and you got stronger."

Ramirez's reaction to my newfound independence was puzzling. Before he went missing I relied on him for everything. He was my protector in life and I needed his strength before I made any moves. Now I knew how to activate the trigger to almost any weapon and I was muscle for a multi-million dollar operation. An operation that he use to run with his brothers.

But when I looked into his eyes I could tell he wasn't the slightest bit intimidated. He fell back in the meetings we had with Bambi and he contributed his opinion when necessary on product, distribution and operation. But he never, ever, over-stepped his boundaries.

"Whatever floats your boat," I smiled. "As long as you remember I'm number one."

He released me and slapped me on the ass. "Woman, I put you before my own life. You already know what it is." He walked away from me.

He sat on the edge of the bed to put his shoes on. Carey sat next to him and he kissed her on the cheek.

"Hurry up, ladies," he said. "Tonight is for us."

"What we celebrating?" I grinned.

"The fact that can't nobody come between our thing," he said seriously. "What we have is special."

"I feel like I'm dreaming," Carey said.

"You are," he replied.

We were in a restaurant with Ramirez, Camp and Dukes from uptown Washington D.C. Why are they even here? I thought it was going to be just the three of us.

Dukes was one of our soldiers out Southwest and I would not have come to dinner if I knew he was going to be there. I don't mix business with pleasure under any circumstances so I was irritated. Ramirez knew that shit. But since he didn't have to work as much because we took over the business, he spent his free time showing off. To make matters worse, Ramirez was on his third drink and he was loud and dumb. If I would've walked up on him and heard him being as ridiculous as he is now, I wouldn't give him the time of day. He was getting major point deductions.

Ramirez was on the right of me, as usual, and Carey was on the left, rubbing my leg under the table. I think she was trying to calm me down because my nigga was draining the life out of me at the moment.

"I'm telling ya'll the new boat Kevin bought not bigger than mine," Ramirez bragged. "I don't care what ya'll nigga's say."

"First off, the nigga bought a Yacht not a boat," Camp said chewing his steak. "He dropped half a million on his shit too. That boat you copped ain't big enough to catch catfish in, moe. You only let three hundred go."

"Cause I got it on a deal," Ramirez said louder. "Ya'll niggas not hearing me though because you stay riding Kevin's dick. Call him up and ask him how much my boat worth. He'll tell you."

"Yeah whatever," Dukes said shaking his head. "You had too much to drink."

Ramirez took a bigger gulp. "Ya'll some jealous ass niggas but I do know something neither one of ya'll got and that includes Kevin."

He waived the waiter over who refreshed his drink. I moved uncomfortably in my seat because he was drinking way too much.

"And what's that?" Camp asked chomping on a piece of bread.

Ramirez looked over at me and slobbed me down. Then he reached across me, grabbed the back of Carey's head and slobbed her down. "Two bad bitches. How 'bout that?" I was done. Why is he kicking our business in the restaurant? It was one thing for him to say it in front of Camp but then we had an employee at our table. Ramirez was out of order. Although I knew everybody was aware of our unique scenario, I didn't want to broadcast it on CNN.

"Ram, chill," I said nudging him like he was some bum nigga in the street. "You doing too much now.

"Baby, you should be proud of this shit right here. Our life is the stuff of legends." He focused his attention on the boys. "Do you know how many niggas envy me right now?"

"I don't give a fuck 'bout what other niggas want," I said harshly. "This ain't me."

"Calm down," he said groping my thigh roughly. "You getting something out of this too. Be proud of it."

"You better chill, man," Camp said. "You know Race a killer now. She don't play the shit she use to. She's all woman."

"Leave the nigga alone," Dukes said eating a cucumber. "Finish telling me how you got it made, Ramirez."

I looked over at Dukes. My stare was long and hard. He didn't know it but tonight would be his last night on earth.

"It's like this," Ramirez said taking the stage again. "Every night when I come home my wife allows me to stick my dick into her and then Carey. Not one of you niggas over here got it like that."

I was so mad I put my hand on my gun and was about to hit my own husband across the temple. I was easing it out of my jeans until Carey placed her warm hand over mine.

"Don't do it," she whispered.

Instead of hitting him, I jumped up from the table and walked toward the bathroom. Carey, who made it clear that she was in my corner over Ramirez's followed me. I pushed the door open and paced the bathroom floor. I felt like committing murder. But what was I mad for? I guess part of me was mad because he played Carey and me in front of them niggas. But the other part of me was mad at how he was putting Carey on display. Before Ramirez left if he did something like this I would've never been so mad at him. What was happening to me now?

Carey, who was wearing this banging ass tight fitting red dress, walked over to me and stopped my motions. "I love you," she said softly. Her breath smelled like strawberries.

"I'm not feeling this nigga right now," I said breathing heavily.

"That nigga you talking about is your husband."

"I know who he is and I still don't give a fuck."

Carey gripped me and pushed me lightly toward the mirror. I was staring at my reflection. I was wearing tight jeans, a tight black shirt and my Jimmy Choo high heels but I felt like a killer.

"Look at yourself. Why are you letting him get to you?"

"Because he trying to play me." I said talking to her through the mirror. "He still think I'm the bitch he met before he left. But I'm different now."

"I know but he's a man, Race. They do dumb shit."

"So I'm supposed to give him a pass?" I paused. "I mean he's out there bragging like I'm letting him do him in this relationship."

"But you are," she said.

"It ain't like that. I don't want people thinking that I allow him to fuck just any old bitch. You in our scenario because I love you and the minute I feel like shit changed you'd be gone."

She looked down and I felt bad but it was the truth. "Wow." She walked away from me. "That hurt."

I walked over to her. "I didn't mean it like that." I rubbed her arm. "You know how I feel about you. I show you everyday. Financially and emotionally."

She sighed. "I hope that's true, Race because I don't know where I would be without you in my life."

"Let's not think about that."

She wiped her hand down her face. "Race, this entire night is getting out of control. What do we care what other people think about our thing? You're both millionaires and you deserve the life you want even if that means having me in it. If other people can't understand it, that's on them." She placed her hand on my face. "Plus I don't want you letting Ramirez think this relationship is about him. You're the queen and king in my book. Now let's walk back out there and remind that nigga."

Damn she knew what to say to me.

"Give me a second." I grabbed my phone out of my pants and called Sarge. When he answered I said, "When you done with them bitches I need you to roll on Dukes. I want him dead by the morning."

"Got it."

I hung up and stuffed my phone back in my pocket.

Carey stood in fear. "Wow, I better never get on your bad side."

I winked, kissed her on the lips and walked back outside to join the fellas. When we got to the table Ramirez was just as loud and ridiculous as he was before I left. He was now on the story of how Carey licked both of our asses clean one night.

I sat next to him and exhaled, while trying to keep a straight face. Dukes was smiling at me until I frowned, forcing him to redirect his glare.

"Ramirez is right," Carey said to everyone at the table after sipping her wine. "There ain't nothing I wouldn't do for them, including fulfilling every one of their needs. It's the only thing I want to do in life."

"And the rich get richer," Camp said with a slight attitude.

"But Ramirez's wrong about one thing," Carey continued jokingly. "I'm Race's toy and he's just along for the ride."

Both Camp and Dukes busted out laughing but Ramirez looked at me as if I were the enemy who just stole his bitch. I winked at him and waived the waiter over to refill my drink.

"Leave the bottle," I told him before he left. "It's really a celebration."

CHAPTER THREE
DENIM

One part of my completely tattooed body was lying on the large beach towel while the other part rested on the hot sand. Bradley eased over me, looked into my eyes and kissed me deeply. I still can't believe after all of these years that our love never waned. Not for one minute.

I had been looking forward to this getaway for weeks. After much planning and preparation we were finally in the Bahamas where we used the time to reconnect and work on our marriage.

When he came back to me, after being gone for so long, it was so much going on at the Kennedy compound that it was bringing down our moods. If Scarlett and Camp weren't arguing, Kevin and Bambi were fussing about the business and the fact that his aunt Bunny was murdered and no one seemed to care. The only one in the house who seemed to be at peace, outside of me, was Race. I'm pretty sure though it had everything to do with the freaky relationship she had going on with Ramirez and Carey.

The tension in the household was exactly why we decided to bounce for a little while. After I took care of business with the Pretty King Empire and we arranged for my mother to watch Jasmine, my hubby and me booked a flight and didn't tell anyone until we landed.

"Denim, I don't know if I told you lately but I'm going to always be in your corner," he said wiping my blue dreads backwards while looking into my eyes. "I know how hard it is for you to juggle the responsibilities of being a mother and what you do with the Pretty Kings Empire. But you doing a great job."

"Baby, it's nothing."

"Now we both know that's not true. But you do make it look easy," he smiled. "I just wanted you to know that no matter what, I'm here. There's nothing more important to me in this world than my wife. I don't take your strength lightly, Denim. You a soldier."

I blushed. "I'm just glad that from the moment you asked me to run away with you that you did right by me. I don't know where or what my life would be like without you."

"You don't have to be glad. It's my responsibility as a man."

"I know, but it's one of the reasons I love you even more. You asked me to marry you and you stayed true."

With everything that was going on I was happy and overwhelmed at the same time. I exhaled. Life was good for me and I should be grateful, but I still feel somewhat empty inside.

"What's on your mind?" he asked me with a serious expression.

"Nothing."

He sat next to me. "Denim, the keeping secrets life ain't for us. In this marriage we keep it real with one another. You know that. Now tell me what's wrong? Let me help you work shit out."

I sat up and looked at the ocean crashing against the yellow sand. "I'm worried about my mother. Lately she been reckless and been letting niggas run up in her like a train in a New York subway station."

"That ain't nothing different. Your mom loves the fellas."

"I know. But the other day I stopped by the house and saw some creepy nigga there who wouldn't say hi. When I asked her who he was she didn't come clean. It was like she was hiding something."

"What do you think it is?"

I looked over at him. "I think she may be prostituting herself."

Bradley laughed and it made me angrier. Wasn't shit about what I said laughable. "What's funny?"

"Wet-Wet," he said brushing my face with the back of his hand. "Sarah been fucking niggas off buck for a minute now."

Bradley calls me Wet-Wet because he said he never met a bitch who had a wetter pussy than mine. And since he was with my sister Grainger before he got with me, I took it as a compliment. Even though to hear her tell it, it was just a matter of time before he went back to her.

"That's some real foul shit to say about my mother, Bradley." I buried my feet into the damp sand. "I know you don't like her, but she's still my mother and she needs me."

"Do you really think your mother's lifestyle is dangerous?"

"Yes, Bradley! What do you think I been saying all along?"

"I hear you but I'm confused. If you really concerned then why is our daughter over her house right now?" I turned away from him and he directed my chin so that my eyes were looking into his. "Don't turn away from me. Jasmine shouldn't be there if you think it's unsafe."

I sighed. "My mother got problems but she not hurting the baby."

"That ain't answering my question, Denim. You know what kind of man I am so I'ma need you to be clearer. Why is she there if you don't trust her? Are you that pressed for a sitter? Because we could've gotten anybody else to do it.

"I let her go over there because my mom says we're keeping Jasmine from her. That's her grandbaby and she has a right to get to know her."

He shook his head. "Jasmine wouldn't recognize your mother if she was holding a nametag."

"Because Jasmine is autistic?" I asked with an attitude.

"No, because your mother isn't necessarily the motherly kind." He paused. "Anyway she doesn't have any rights, Denim."

I frowned. "So because there ain't no law she shouldn't be able to see her? What kind of shit is that?"

"You know I ain't saying that shit. I'm just saying there ain't no law saying we gotta let her see our daughter. And that any time she does share with Jasmine she better cherish. What you need to understand is that I'll do anything to protect you and my daughter. And if that means not letting her go with your mother to keep her safe then so be it. Now is she safe over there or not?"

"Of course, Bradley. My mother would never let anything happen to Jasmine."

"For your sake I hope not."

I turned around and faced him. "So you threatening me now?"

"It ain't about threatening. I will hurt anybody who hurts either of you, and that goes for blood relatives too."

"You don't care about my mother do you?"

"Who don't care about your mother?" he pointed at himself. "Didn't I just drop five stacks on the gastric bypass surgery she underwent? I care about her but not at the expense of my kid or my family."

When my phone rang I took it out of the off-white Polo beach bag and removed it. When I saw my mother's name I sighed.

"Speak of the devil," I said to Bradley. I showed him the screen.

"Well let me go grab a beer from the cooler. You 'bout to be on the phone with her for an hour."

"No I'm not either." I playfully hit him on the shoulder as he got up to move toward the red cooler a few feet over from us.

Pressing the phone against my ear I asked, "What's up, ma?"

"You gonna be mad at me," she responded. "Before you kill me I ask that you just hear me out."

I rolled my eyes as I watched Bradley digging through the cooler. "What you do this time? Let another guy fuck you and leave you butt naked in the new house I bought you?"

"Why you always gotta say smart shit outta your face, child? I'm still your mother."

"Go 'head, ma," I sighed. "I'm trying to enjoy my vacation."

"Anyway it ain't about none of that. It's about Jasmine."

My heart rocked in my chest and I leapt up. Bradley was walking back toward me with a beer in his hand until he saw the fear on my face. The can fell out of his hand and rolled in the sand.

"What happened to my baby, ma?" I yelled. "What the fuck you do to my baby?"

CHAPTER FOUR
BAMBI

I was in the backyard of the cottage my sisters and me bought before my husband showed back up. We didn't stay here unless we were trying to get away because my sons preferred the Kennedy compound.

I was wearing a white wifebeater with my fatigue pants and because I was sweating my clothes clung to my skin. I just finished burying money on the property and was patting the dirt with the bottom of the shovel to flatten it.

When I was done I threw the shovel on the ground and wiped the sweat off my dirty face with the back of my hand.

I looked over at Kevin who was sitting on a tree stump a few feet over from me drinking a beer. "I told you I could help you," he said.

"You said you would but I could tell you didn't really want to." I walked over to him.

"What you talking about now?" he said with a smirk on his face.

"I'm talking about you letting me dig the hole and fill it back up to bury the cash by myself. I mean what's wrong with you? It's obvious you got something against me."

"I don't have anything against you," he responded. "Stop tripping. What I would like to know is why you keep burying money back here? There are other places you know."

"You mean the places the government knows about?" I asked rolling my eyes. "You just being lazy then?"

He laughed. "Lazy? I'm just letting you do what you obviously want to do anyway—be a man."

I walked over to him and sat at his feet. I was done arguing with him. I wanted us to have the type of relationship that Denim and Bradley had. I wanted us to be in love again. I placed my head on his knees and exhaled. He rubbed my hair softly and I could smell the beer on his breath. The crickets sang in the background and the partially wet grass was dampening my pants.

"I'm sorry, Bambi. I know I haven't been myself since I came back. I got so much going on in my mind and sometimes I don't put you on to it all."

"But why?"

"Because I don't wanna sound like I'm nagging. If I told you everything you would probably leave me."

I raised my head and looked up at him. "Never, Kevin. Don't you know that about me yet?"

He smiled and I placed my head back on his knee. He ran his rough fingers along the side of my cheek.

"Talk to me, Kevin," I said. "Please. I'm still your wife and I love you. All I want to know is what I can do to make things right for you. No matter what it is I'm going to do it. Do you want to run the operation again? I don't have any problem stepping down."

"Even if I wanted to, Mitch ain't trying to hear from me right now. You know how he is when he builds a connection. Even though the white boy knew me before you were even my wife, he talks to me like I'm a stranger."

"So you did talk to him?" I asked.

I was disappointed that he felt he had to go around me to get at Mitch. I never once told him that I didn't respect him as the head of our operation. So why go over my head?

"I tried to talk to him and he told me if I wanted any info on the business that I gotta go through you."

"And that's my fault?"

"Kinda," he yelled.

I took my head off his knee and looked up at him. I wanted him to know that I was trying to make this marriage work, but I needed him to meet me half way. It seemed like every time we spoke now it was business related.

"Kevin, I'm sorry Mitch ain't trying to talk about the details of the coke shipments with you. But when I thought you were killed I needed to do what I had to do to take care of our family. So I got up with your connect but it wasn't easy. Look at the scars on my face. I paid for the relationship I have with him in blood. Them Russians wanted Mitch's information so badly they tortured me and still I didn't bend."

"I know," he said in a frustrated tone.

"Do you really?" I paused. "If the shoes were on the other foot would you have been able to deal with them punching you in the face? Or beating you with poles and their belt buckles? Or better yet stabbing you?"

"Calm down, Bambi. You going too far."

"I won't calm down. I need you to know that the scar on my face wasn't easy. Mitch wouldn't deal with me at first until he found out everything I had gone through to protect him. I can't help it if he doesn't want to work personally with you or your brothers again. It ain't like I'm not involving you in the business anyway."

"I'm just worried that you so close to the business. It's dangerous."

"And I can handle myself," I said.

He looked at me and rubbed his hand over the scars over my face. I took several slashes to my face with a knife. Despite Kevin and everybody else telling me I was beautiful, after what the Russians did to me I was left with a constant reminder that I sacrificed my looks for business and my family.

"I know you keep me posted on what's going on but it's not the same, Bambi."

"Then what do you want me to do? Why are you afraid to say it?" I stood up, brushed the back of my pants and looked down at him. "I can't teach you how to feel masculine again just because I'm running—"

"What makes you think I'm not feeling masculine?" he said with an attitude interrupting me.

"Because you stiff, Kevin. Ever since you been back you been stiff and lifeless. And I want my husband back. I want my best friend back."

Kevin drank the rest of his beer and threw the can on the ground. He stood up and walked toward me. "What happened to my aunt Bunny?"

The question came from nowhere and I felt like the life had been drained from me. If there was one topic I hated talking about, aunt Bunny was it.

"What you mean?"

"I mean what happened to her? What really happened? Why is everyone, including my boys, afraid to talk about the fact that she was murdered in her house?"

"It's not that we don't want to talk to you about it. It's just that whenever the topic is up for more than five minutes you get angry."

"That's because she's the only woman who really loved me."

I frowned. "So what am I?"

"I didn't mean it like that. I'm just…"

"Worried about something that can't be changed," I said finishing his sentence. "She's gone, Kevin and I know it hurts you but it's the truth."

"It just fucks me up that's all. I never got to say good-bye. What happened, Bambi? I feel you know something but you holding back."

"This is what I'm talking about. The family is afraid to talk about Bunny because we can't provide you with any more information than what we already have. All any of us knows is that somebody robbed her, ran up in the house, stole her chain and killed her."

"I wish I knew who took that chain. If I knew who took the chain I would be able to find her killer too."

My heart rate increased even more. Not only was I aware who took his aunt Bunny's chain, I also knew who killed her. It was all me. That dirty, old bitch died by my hands when she tried to get in the way of a major deal that was going down with The Russians. I didn't wanna kill her, but Bunny pushed me into a corner and I came out in attack mode. In the end, it became her life or my money and she lost.

The worst part about it is that before she died she alluded to having a sexual relationship with her own nephew, Kevin. Part of me knew it was because she was trying to hurt me and remind me that Kevin loved her more than he did me. But the other part of me believed her and I had a small seed of hate in my heart for Kevin.

"You really need to let it go, Kevin. It's time to move on with our lives. You home now and—"

"Did you have something to do with my aunt's death?"

"Do you really think I could be that cold?" I placed my hand over my heart. "Is that what you think of me? Bunny and me had our beef but I didn't hate her and I wouldn't hurt her. Why would you even ask me something like that?"

He dropped his head. "I know you didn't do it, sweetheart. I'm sorry about how I been coming at you lately. My mind is messed up and I feel like I don't know who I can trust. Even though I know now that the nigga who came up in the casino had nothing to do with my brothers and me, at one point I thought it was a hit. I thought somebody was out to get me. I thought it was you because you found out about my son."

He was right on some part. I was going to kill him but when he was almost murdered I realized I loved him and wanted him alive. It was a close call but that serial killer saved his life.

"Well you're wrong," I responded. I put my hand on the side of his face. "You're safe now."

He was looking at me but I could tell he was thinking about something else. "If I find out who killed my aunt it won't be good." He focused on me and I dropped my hand. "It's important that you know that."

"I know, baby. I know. And if I find out who did it my gun gonna be right beside yours."

CHAPTER FIVE

SCARLETT

A FEW DAYS LATER

The sound of classical music played in the air as Ngozi fucked me hard in the men's restroom on a public bathroom toilet. We were in the mall when he said the urge to have sex with me hit him so hard that he couldn't hold off until we made it back to the hotel room I rented for us.

Since he was sitting on the toilet bowl, my back was faced him as I rode his dick. I felt slutty but that was one of the reasons I agreed to do it. I knew Camp would be devastated if he saw me like this. I knew it would break his heart even if he claimed he didn't want to be with me anymore. After all, I was still his pregnant wife. He would never be able to stomach that the baby I was carrying in my belly was with me as I gave another man the pussy.

"Fuck this dick you pretty white bitch," Ngozi said in a heavy African accent. He pumped into me so hard that it felt like I was on one of them mechanical bulls. "I'm going to fill you up so that you remember my name. And who this pussy belongs too."

"Give it to me," I encouraged. "Give it all to me, baby."

I placed my hand on his thighs and bit down on my bottom lip. When I looked down to the floor I was staring at the brown leather Christian Louboutin tennis I bought him and my red high heels. Crumpled tissue and drops of urine puddles were everywhere around us.

I didn't care how disgusting everything was. All I knew was that my pussy tingled and I was on the verge of cumming. Damn he knew how to make me feel. He knew what I liked and he didn't mind giving it to me. Rough or soft. Maybe that's one of the reasons I tricked on him so hard.

Money was not a problem although I hated when he asked me for it. I preferred to give it to him freely because I wanted him to have it. It was as if he was my possession and I owned him. There was something else that bothered me about him. Although he always wanted money I couldn't help but wonder if there was something else he wanted from me. Something he wasn't telling me.

Ngozi placed his hands on the side of my stomach and pushed into me so hard I could feel my baby kicking around again. I should've stopped him but I wanted to mentally escape from my world.

Earlier today Bambi made a huge breakfast for everyone. The entire time Camp was sitting at the table judging me. Looking at me and making me feel like a slut. He wanted me to know how he felt about me and he wanted our family to know too. The marriage was over and I knew it. I didn't even want to go home anymore.

"This my pussy right, Scarlett," Ngozi asked. "Tell me it's mine."

"Fuck me harder," I responded ignoring his question.

Ngozi pounded into me so hard my head banged against the stall door. I was moaning and making so much noise I knew people heard us.

"Hey, what are ya'll doing in there?" someone yelled on the outside.

"What does it sound like we're doing?" Ngozi responded while still pumping into my body. "We're fucking," he laughed.

"Well I'm going to get security! This is an outrage."

When he left Ngozi and I laughed.

"You better hurry up," I whispered to him. "Before he—"

My sentence was cut short when I felt a warm sensation streaming between my legs. When I looked down a murky like fluid spilled out on the bathroom floor. Suddenly Ngozi's thighs were moist and the floor was soaked.

"What the fuck is that," he asked. "Did you just piss on me?"

"Ngozi, I think my water just broke."

"What? How did that happen?"

"I don't know." I looked down at the floor again. "Maybe it got something to do with how rough we're being."

I rubbed my lower belly. Suddenly I was in the realization that I was a pregnant woman and shouldn't be going so hard just to get back at Camp.

"Your water didn't break," he told me as if he were an unsympathetic doctor. "Just relax. Besides, this is a fantasy of mine and I'm having a good time."

"You gotta stop, Ngozi! "

"But I didn't cum yet."

I turned my head around and looked at him. When I tried to move he kept pulling me back down. "Ngozi, I'm in labor. I have to go to the hospital. The game is over."

He looked at me and it was as if his face transformed. He wasn't the same person I had come to know in the past. He looked demonic. Like he didn't care for my baby or me. I was horrified because it felt like I was sharing my body with a complete stranger all this time and didn't know it.

"Did you hear what I said, bitch? I didn't cum yet. Now turn your head back around so I can finish before you have that baby in this bathroom. I'm gonna be quick."

He smooched my face real hard, which forced my head frontwards. His dick continued to pump in and out of me roughly. I couldn't believe he was doing this. He was being beyond selfish. I was experiencing waves of pain throughout my belly and my head throbbed. I didn't want my baby entering into the world with a man's sperm on his crown, but what could I do? I didn't want to admit it but he was raping me.

———————

I finally made it to the hospital. My feet were sitting in the cool black stirrups. My knees touched the sides of my belly as I pushed with all of my might. The doctor stood in front of me as he coached the baby out of my body. Two nurses were at his side and giving me all of the support they could. But still something felt off. There was one person who shouldn't be here. But there he was holding my hand as if he hadn't raped me not even two hours earlier.

"I see the crown of the baby's head," Dr. Morgan advised me. "Don't give up. Just keep pushing."

As I continued to push all I kept thinking about was my husband. I wondered where he was and what he was doing. I realized at that moment that I did want to try again even if he didn't want to. I just needed to get rid of Ngozi. I'm such an emotional mess. So confused.

"You're doing good, Mrs. Kennedy," the black nurse said as she smiled down at me. "Just keep breathing."

Her warm eyes made me feel safe and I needed her because there was a demon at my bedside.

"The baby is coming," the doctor coached. "I can see his head. Just keep pushing."

I bore down with all of my might. And since Ngozi held my hand and refused to let go I tried to crush the bones in his fingers. He tried to snatch away from me but I didn't let him go.

You wanted to be here so be here, bitch. I thought to myself.

It was because of him I had to have this baby with no anesthesia. By the time I made it to the hospital the baby was already coming and it was too dangerous to give me an epidural.

I pushed and pushed until I saw the doctor holding my baby in his arms. I knew at that moment when I saw his little penis that it was a boy. The doctor placed him into my arms and I kissed him on the head. He was perfect. My tiny baby was perfect.

The doctor grinned as if Ngozi were the father. "So what's his name?"

I wiped my finger over his forehead. "Master. His name is Master Kennedy."

CHAPTER SIX
KEVIN

Kevin and Cloud were watching a basketball game while drinking beer on the living room sofa at Cloud's house. They were cousins who didn't always see eye to eye but they tried to get along. One of the main reasons Kevin didn't like him was because he had an idea that Cloud was in love with his wife Bambi. But they were blood and Kevin took blood seriously.

"So how are things at home?" Cloud asked while looking at the TV. "I know it's been some time since you been back."

"Home is home," he said flatly.

Cloud looked over at him. "What does that mean?"

"It means that even though I'm back and it hasn't even been a year, so much has changed. I don't know her anymore. It's hard for our marriage, man."

"Of course you do. It ain't like she's still not your wife."

"I know she's my wife but things are different now."

Cloud popped the top to another beer. "Explain."

"For starters she takes a lot of late night calls. And when I ask her who she's talking to she says its business related."

"Maybe it is. She is running the operation."

"I know my wife. I mean I really know my wife. I can tell when she's about to get her period three days before it comes just by the smell of her pussy. So trust me when I tell you that something is different."

"You think she's cheating?"

"I don't know if it's that or if it's something else. You know? Whatever it is I do know I'm not feeling it."

"So what are you going to do?"

"I'm gonna play it by ear but I do know this, if I find out she's fucking another man I'm going to kill her and then I'm going to kill him." he looked over at Cloud as if he were speaking directly to him. *"You feel me?"*

CHAPTER SEVEN
SCARLETT

My baby boy was beautiful but something strange happened once he was here. I realized I didn't want a child. The feeling was strong and precise. Not even three hours later I felt disconnected. I told myself it was postpartum depression but I really couldn't say for sure.

Maybe if I saw my husband I would feel differently and I couldn't wait for him to see Master and hug him. But there was one problem. I had Ngozi, and now his mother, Abebi inside of my room smiling like Master was in their bloodline.

"You are blessed, Abebi," said to me. She had a beautiful gold and blue scarf tied around her head with a matching dress. "To be able to give birth is a gift from the Gods. It means you are special and you are to never forget that. Ever."

I smiled through the frown. I didn't know this woman and wanted her and her sick ass son away from me. Why were they still here? Why wouldn't they leave me alone? Part of me wanted to contact the police but the other part was too embarrassed. Not only that, I have warrants for some shit I did years ago and couldn't risk getting caught.

After Ngozi raped me on the bathroom toilet when I told him I was going into labor I knew our relationship was done.

Besides with the baby I wasn't going to be able to hang out with him no more. I had responsibilities now.

"Thank you," I said to his mother.

"No. Thank the Gods."

I nodded. This chick was getting weirder by the second.

"Ngozi," I said softly. "Can I talk to you? In private? It's really important."

Ngozi looked at his mother and said something to her in his native tongue again. She looked over at me. This time she didn't have a smile on her face. It was more like a smirk. Abedi always gave me the creeps because she practiced a faith that I didn't like.

When I was coming up my grandmother and aunt practiced Black Magic. She would have parties at her house where she and her friends would come over and they would put hexes on people they didn't like. I shared my fear with Ngozi a few weeks after we got together. He told me all about his family but he never mentioned that his mother practiced Voodoo until a week ago.

Ngozi spent countless hours telling me how his mother's co-workers were dropping left and right after having disagreements with her. He seemed proud that whatever she wanted she got and whoever didn't agree with her was wrong.

A few stories scared me but there was one that made me not want to be around her— ever. One day Abebi got angry with one of her co-workers at Subtle Sanitation Services, when the woman was offered a promotion over her. Ngozi said she invoked Ti Jean Quinto, a mean African spirit who lives under bridges and assumes the form of a policeman.

In one month, her co-worker lost the promotion, her job, her husband to divorce, and she was stricken with a bout of cervix cancer, which eventually took her life. I learned from the beginning to fear Abebi and I always did.

Abebi walked over to me, placed her hand on my forehead and said something in African. Her voice was loud and rocked my core. A nurse walking by looked into the room until Abedi gave her the evil eye.

What did Abedi say over me?

"I'm leaving now, sweetheart," she said in English. It was as if she were now an entirely different person. "I understand that you want to be alone with my son and I will give you that time." She ran the back of her hand alongside my face. "And don't look so sad. I'll be back later to check on you. Okay?"

I nodded hoping she would leave right away. What was her obsession with me? It wasn't like I was his girlfriend or that the baby was Ngozi's. Her and I had no business together so you might as well say I was just a jump off.

I watched her high headscarf bend the corner before I finally breathed a sigh of relief. One irritant down and one more to go.

"You look irritated with me," he said.

"Can you tell?

"Why are you angry?"

He was playing me closely. I was starting to wonder if he was afraid that because he raped me in the bathroom, that I would not want to be bothered with him any more. He was right.

"Ngozi, I'm fine and there's nothing wrong. All I wanted to say to you is that I'm better and you can leave now."

He walked up to the bed and smiled. "And why would I leave you now? That's not like me."

"You should leave because I had the baby already and all I want to do is get some rest."

"But you're alone in this world, Scarlett. Even with all of those people around you. Besides I'm from Africa and the men in my country would never abandon you in this time of need. So I won't either. Now you can rest and I'll be by your side when you awaken."

I can't believe he's doing this. He's acting like he didn't just take advantage of me even though I begged him not to. "Ngozi, let's not play games. You raped me in the bathroom and I can't stand the sight of you anymore. Now if you want me to consider you at all in the future I need you to allow me the time I need to think about our relationship."

"I didn't rape you," he said flatly. "You gave me your body willingly and I accepted. So what are you going to do? Be the kind of woman to sleep with a black man and then scream rape?"

"Ngozi!"

"I'm simply asking a question."

He had me so angry I was huffing and puffing. I needed to calm down before I sent my pressure into overdrive.

"You did rape me. I told you I was going into labor and you wouldn't let me go. Remember? I don't know about your country but in America, white or black, that's still rape."

"You and I are meant to be, Scarlett. And there aren't many things that can change that. Although I do know a few."

Many things? What does that mean?

This was a complete nightmare. I shook my head and lowered it. He wasn't going anywhere and I knew it now for sure. If I called the cops I would be the white woman who fucked a black man and yelled rape. I could also be arrested. But if I didn't say anything he would take up too much time and I wouldn't be able to call Camp. I was confused.

"What did your mother say over me?" I asked him when I remembered she spoke something in her native language.

"She invoked the LOA Captain Debas spirit. He was a good person who stood for family. Essentially she is saying that we are going to be together, forever, until we both die. And if I should die before you, your soul will quickly follow mine."

CHAPTER EIGHT
DENIM

My vacation was over early but it seemed like it took us forever to get back home. I still can't believe that my stupid-irresponsible-ass mother let Jasmine swallow a pen top because she wasn't watching her.

All she said was, "You gotta come home now!"

Had it not been for Bambi going to make sure she was okay I would be a nervous wreck. They were able to get the top out of her throat right after she choked, luckily for her. Bambi asked me did I want her to pick Jasmine up but I said I would be back the next day so she was fine there.

I was sitting outside in the car with my husband. From the passenger seat, under the night sky, I glanced over at the house I bought for my mother in the suburbs of Maryland. The funny thing is, I don't even have a house of my own. For some reason the eight of us (The Kennedy Klan) feel more comfortable living together even though I wasn't sure how long that would last.

Unlike my sisters I want to be alone with my husband. I want to see how it would be to have our own spot. But when I brought it up to Bradley he said that instead of moving away from the family he would rather buy a bigger mansion. A place so large that we wouldn't have to see the others unless we wanted to.

Although I'm sitting in the passenger seat looking at my mother's house, I want nothing more than to go inside and choke the shit out of her for almost killing my daughter. I know me though. Once I start the violent streak there's no stopping me.

"Baby, I don't want you to go in there and let them set you off," Bradley said placing a soft hand on my thigh. "You have to be smart when you dealing with your people. You know how it is."

"That's easy for you to say."

"What you talking 'bout?"

"You don't have to deal with them like I do. They're my selfish ass family and they're my problem."

"That's because you make it that way."

"I'm serious, Bradley. It's like I do everything I can for my mother and she can't do anything right for me. I'm sick of this shit. I mean look at the house she living in." I looked at the five hundred thousand dollar brick home. "I bought that for her but does she appreciate it? Fuck no."

"If you tired of being used than stop it. I mean what else do you want me to say? I agree with you but I also have to tell you that I hear this all the time. One minute you tired of your mother but the next minute she needs you and you drop everything and go. Stop letting her use you, baby."

I exhaled and looked down at his hand. "But she's my mother," I said in a whisper. "And I love her."

He removed his hand and leaned back into the driver's seat. The leather seat groaned. "Denim, I don't know why you feel just because she's your mother that you have to eat her shit. You my wife and —"

"You don't have to deal with this," I said finishing his sentence. I looked over at him. "I know that's true. I just want my mother to realize how much I love her and I want her to start appreciating me."

"She's not going to appreciate you unless you give her a reason to. You have to set your bottom lines and stick by them, babes." He rubbed my face with the back of his hand. "I wish I could take this pressure off you, Denim. Tell me what I can do."

I looked over at my husband. When he said he loved me I believed him. I felt it whenever he was in the room. I often spent days wondering why he loved me so much. I don't think he really knew. Whenever I asked him he said he wasn't sure, but something told me we were together in a past life and reunited in this one.

"Just you being here with me is all I need, baby." I squeezed his hand. "I don't know who I would be if you weren't in my life. It's like our souls are connected. Intertwined."

"I hear you talking that fly shit," he joked.

"I'm serious. All I need is you."

He looked over at the house and I followed his gaze. "Denim, you know I'm not going anywhere. Not even a death threat could keep me away. Trust me." He looked at the house. "But look, before we go inside I wanna say something. Don't let Grainger or your mother get you out of character."

"Bradley, I'm not trying to—"

"You hear me?" he yelled interrupting me.

He looked into my eyes and I had to admit. I'ma tough bitch but I love when he's in control. I feel safe.

"I hear you," I said submitting.

He exhaled again. "Good." He rubbed my thigh again. "Well let's get this shit over with so we can enjoy the rest of our night."

We got out of the car and I lazily walked over to the house. I used my key and entered, my husband was right behind me. The moment the door opened the smell of funk hit my face. When I looked down I was disgusted. There was large green trash bags lined up against the wall, lint on the plush gray carpets and dirty clothes everywhere my eyes could land. How could my mother and sister treat a luxury home like a dumpster?

"What the fuck is up with your moms?" Bradley asked. "I thought our maid came over here once a week to clean up their spot too."

"I guess she hasn't been able to get in."

All I could do was shake my head. If she wanted to live in the projects, I could grant her wish and send her back.

I walked toward the back of the house and Grainger was bending the corner holding my daughter's hand. Grainger's hair was sectioned in tiny black twists and I could tell she was trying to dread her hair like mine. Anything to be like me I guess. The white t-shirt she was wearing was stained with brown spots and she was sporting a pair of dark blue holey sweatpants. She looked a hot ass mess. I guess she was still fucking with that heroin after all.

I quickly grabbed my daughter and gave her to Bradley. He picked her up and hugged her before placing her back down. Jasmine babbled like she normally does since she suffers from Autism. Although recently we took her to a new doctor who changed her meds and we noticed a slight difference in her behavior, but she still wasn't interacting with me like I wanted. The new doctor said we should see an even greater change soon. I hope he's right.

I focused back on Grainger. "Where ma at?" I looked behind her.

She placed her hands on her hips before folding her arms over her chest. "She not here. And it's about time you got here to pick up Jasmine. I had something to do you know. It ain't like you paying me to babysit."

I frowned. I told my mother I didn't want my daughter being alone with Grainger. I didn't trust her. Why should I? She was angry that I was with Bradley, her ex-boyfriend and she resented our marriage. God only knew what she would do to my baby.

"For your information I didn't want to watch her either. It's not my fault ma got up with one of her boyfriends."

Every time she opened her mouth I could see her fucked up teeth. I guess from all of the years of doing dope.

"Why the fuck would she leave?" I said to no one in particular. "I told her I was on my way. Plus I wanted to talk to her to find out why she left Jasmine by herself. She's only five and she's autistic so what the fuck was on her mind?"

"You know how ma is when she gets a new dick. She jumps on it."

"Watch your language in front of my daughter," Bradley told her. "And if my mouth looked like yours I wouldn't say much."

She gave him an evil look. A long look. In that moment I could tell she hated him for what he took away from her in the life he provided for me. But Bradley was never meant for her and although it was wrong we were happily in love.

Still he hit her where it hurt the most when he brought up her mouth. She was self-conscious about her missing teeth and he knew it.

"My bad, Bradley," she said sarcastically. She tried to pull her top lip down as she spoke to hide her teeth. "I forgot how you feel about your precious little baby."

"Grainger, why you so ignorant?" I asked. "If you hate me so much why are you living in the house that I bought? Go out in the world and do you. Trust me, nobody here will stop you."

"This ma's house. Not yours!"

"Bitch, my name is on this mortgage. And I allowed you to stay here with her if you took care of her." I looked around at the filth. "Yet the house is a mess and my daughter almost died."

Grainger laughed. "You are so fucking dry, Denim. You always coming at me about that retarded ass baby of yours. Can't nobody fuck up that kid more than it's fucked up already."

By the time I went to grab her and snatch some sense into her I saw a blur roll past the side of my face. It was Bradley's fist and it landed directly into my sister's mouth. Grainger dropped to the floor and I could tell she didn't have use of her lower mouth because her tongue rolled around.

Oh my God! I think Bradley just cracked her jaw.

CHAPTER NINE
RACE

I was in front of my floor length mirror wearing my yellow lace bra and panty set. I was watching Ramirez and Carey kiss in the bed. First he was asking me how I felt about her and the next minute he was team Carey again. I was confused. We just finished fucking before I got the call that Scarlett had the baby. I was about to tell him about his nephew being born but he was occupied.

As I was sliding into my jeans Carey said, "Race, please come back to bed. We were just getting started."

I grinned. "I can't fuck with it now. My sister just called and said she had her baby."

"Oh snap, Scarlett had the kid?" Ramirez said finally looking at me and coming up for air. "I know Camp gonna be flipping."

"Yep." I nodded.

"Want me to roll with you?"

I appreciated him asking but Scarlett was firm about not bringing the fellas.

"I got it, baby. I'll hit you later."

I don't know what was going on with her but I had plans to find out. I kissed both of them, grabbed my purse and my gun and walked out.

When I made it to the hospital parking lot and got out of my Porsche I saw Denim and Jasmine rushing toward the entrance. She was in a hurry and I didn't understand why. Scarlett already had the baby so what was going on? Her energy put me on edge because I knew something was up.

I walked up to her right before she made it to Scarlett's room and said, "You cool?"

"It's a long story, Race." She turned around to leave. "I'll rap to you about it later."

I snatched her by the arm and pulled her back around. "Bitch, tell me what's going on now. How you gonna do that shit to me? You know how bad my nerves are. What's up with you?"

"Let's just say Grainger is in another room in this hospital because Bradley broke her jaw."

I released her arm and my mouth hung open. She walked ahead of me and I looked at her as I shook my head. I didn't know Bradley to have a violent side. He seemed to be all Denim and no hate. I guess I was wrong.

Although I can't authenticate no nigga hitting no bitch, I know what kind of mouth Grainger is working with. I almost bust her in the teeth a few times myself when I heard the slick shit she said behind Denim's back.

When the three of us made it to Scarlett's hospital room I saw Ngozi and Bambi inside. I hugged Scarlett and read her face like it was a newspaper. It didn't take me long to realize what was going on. This nigga was unwanted and she didn't know how to get rid of him. I guess that's where we came in.

I walked up to him and said, "We appreciate you coming out, Ngozi. And being there for her while she had the baby, but we got her from here."

"I'm good," he said in a heavy African accent. "I don't mind staying."

Let me be clear on a few things. I never fucked with this dude. In my opinion he mooched off of Scarlett and took advantage of the fact that she was lonely and pregnant. But what could I say when I was bedding a husband and a mistress every night?

"She's right," Bambi said coming in on his right, as Denim caught the left and I stood tall in his face. "You can leave. Family is in the building now."

When he acted like he was about to get fly with Bambi I stabbed the barrel of my gun in his crotch.

"I know you not about to say nothing you gonna regret," I warned him. "It would be a wrong move. For you and any future children you desire to have."

He looked at me, Bambi, Denim and then Scarlett. He walked out without saying a word. The fact that he said nothing made me worried but I knew we could deal with him later if he got out of hand.

I walked over to the bed. "How you feeling?" I asked Scarlett holding her pale hand inside of mine.

"Not good at all."

"What the fuck is up with dude?" Denim asked as Jasmine stuffed the edge of Scarlett's bed sheet in her mouth before Bambi took it out. "Why Ngozi acting all weird and shit."

"I'm not feeling him no more and I don't know what to say to him," Scarlett replied. She seemed frustrated.

"Tell him it's over," I said. "It ain't rocket science."

She sighed. "It's not that easy."

"Why isn't it?" Bambi asked sitting on the edge of the bed while touching her leg. "You had fun with him and now you want him the fuck out of your life. It's not hard to me. Plus you got a baby now. The last thing you need is to be keeping time with some creepy ass man from Africa."

"I don't trust him," she said in a soft voice. "I got a feeling he's going to try and hurt me."

"Then I'll have him killed," Bambi said plainly.

"I'm on it," I responded ready to place the death order with Sarge.

"No," Scarlett yelled. "I mean...please don't do that. Not yet anyway."

"Do you got love for this dude or not?" I asked.

"I don't have love for him but...I mean...I'm so confused..."

"Then tell us what you want us to do." I said. "Because what we not about to do is sit around and let somebody scare you a darker shade of red. You got too much power behind you to be afraid of any man, beast or thing. And I know you know that."

"She's right," Bambi responded. "One word and he'll be ground beef."

She smiled. "I love you guys. Always ready to kill somebody."

"We know you love us," Bambi said. "Which is why we want to keep you around a little while longer." She paused. "Now what's up with Camp? Why he not here to see his baby?"

"I wanted Ngozi out first," she said. "He was chilling in here like Master was his son."

"Wait, you named the baby, Master?" Bambi asked excitedly. "That shit's dope!"

Scarlett smiled. "Thank you. I figured Camp would like it too." She paused and looked down at the bed then back at Bambi. "You mind calling him for me, Bambi? I think he'll like hearing it better from you."

"Why don't you call your own husband?" She asked playfully. "You know that man gonna be excited when he learns he has a son. He'll want to hear it from you not his sister-in-law."

"Let's keep it real. You know he's not feeling me right now."

She shook her head. "Sometimes these niggas are the death of us." Bambi stood up and grabbed her phone out of her purse. "But of course I'll call him for you."

While Bambi got on the phone with Camp, Scarlett looked over at Denim. "I know you just got back from vacation so I appreciate you coming over. Where's Bradley at?"

Denim sighed. "I've already told Race so I guess I'll tell ya'll too. Bradley hit Grainger and broke her jaw."

"Oh my, God," Scarlett said covering her mouth. "Why?"

"You know how my sister is. She said some fly shit out her mouth about Jasmine and he reacted in her defense. So he's gonna stay away from the house because he got a feeling Grainger gonna snitch."

"By snitch do you mean go to the police?" Scarlett asked with raised eyebrows.

"For her sake I hope she doesn't," I responded. "It would be un-good."

"Grainger is my sister but I wouldn't even stand in the way of that order," Denim replied. "Not when it comes to my husband. I will just help put flowers over her early grave."

CHAPTER TEN
BAMBI

I'm standing next to the bed looking at Scarlett as she holds her beautiful baby lovingly in her arms. Denim was sitting on the bed smiling, while Race was making baby noises as she rubbed Master's cheek. I'm probably the only one not with this shit. It doesn't feel right that Scarlett had another baby.

I never told Scarlett to her face because I didn't think she could handle it, but I never wanted her to go through with the pregnancy. One of the reasons I tolerated Ngozi for as long as I did was because secretly I hoped he would cause her to have a miscarriage. Maybe beat it out of her or something. Then we could kill him.

I know it's cruel but Scarlett with a baby is also dangerous. Real dangerous. And I'm scared of what might happen if she's left to care for Master alone. I have a good reason for feeling that way.

One day Scarlett was left alone to watch Denim's daughter when she needed an emergency babysitter. Usually when she needed someone to watch Jasmine either Race or I would do it. When we weren't available she would go to her mother. But Denim couldn't get any of us that day so she begged Scarlett, who everyone knew didn't like children. That was a major mistake.

Scarlett wasn't with Jasmine for longer than two hours before I received a frantic call. Scarlett said she was bathing Jasmine when she accidently fell with the baby and broke her leg on the edge of the tub. Although I was willing to give Scarlett the benefit of the doubt, Denim had her suspicions. She said that Scarlett never wanted to watch Jasmine so she hurt her on purpose.

Scarlett always said that it was an accident but I knew a secret she didn't tell my sisters. Camp thought she was only married to him but Scarlett told me that she was married before. I also knew that she was abusive to a daughter that she and her ex-husband had together, which was why she ran away from her old life into ours. Although I promised to keep Scarlett's secret, I also demanded that she get help for her problems. Now that she had Master I was going to see to it that she kept her vow.

"What about the warrants?" I whispered to Scarlett.

"I don't think they report babies being born to the police. Hopefully I won't get locked up."

Scarlett had a warrant for her arrest for a crime she committed with her first husband. It's for child abuse against her daughter. She was due in court to answer to the abuse charges and never showed up. Instead she met Camp that same day and had been with him ever since. She was a tortured soul.

I sighed. "Well where is Camp?" I asked her looking at my watch. "He should've been here by now."

"Did you reach him?"

"It went to voicemail."

Scarlett looked up at me and sighed.

"He doesn't care," she said softly. "He doesn't care about me anymore and I don't know what to do."

I felt bad for her. I knew even though she was fucking the African dude that her heart really lied with her husband. But the way she was going about getting Camp back was messy and wouldn't work in her favor. I was sure of it.

"Things will work out," I responded. "That's all I'm going to say."

The baby started crying and Scarlett moved awkwardly around in the bed. The baby's wail got louder and Scarlett seemed more frustrated. Afraid she was five seconds from tossing the baby into the wall I picked him up from her. She looked up at me and the distraught look on her face softened. She appeared calmer. I rocked the baby in my arms for five seconds before he quieted down. He was adorable.

The nurse walked into the room. "Okay, it's time for us to check his vitals." She smiled at him while he lay in my arms. "I'll bring him right back when I'm done."

"No," Scarlett yelled. She must've realized how crazy she sounded so she looked at all of us and lowered her head. In a low voice she said, "I mean, you don't have to bring him back right away. I'm kind of tired."

I handed Master to the nurse and she cradled the baby in her arms. "I understand. Most new mothers tire easy. I'll be back with Master later on tonight. You get some rest, dear."

Scarlett nodded and smiled. "Thank you."

When the nurse left and we were alone everything was silent for a moment. I wish I knew what was on my sisters' minds. Did they think Scarlett was acting as weird as I did?

"Like Bambi said, where the fuck is Camp?" Race asked breaking the silence. "He should've been here by now. This nigga just had a son. A cutie pie at that."

"Can you call him for me again?" Scarlett asked me.

"I'll call the nigga," Race said grabbing her phone out of her purse. "If I have to grab him by his dick he will come see his kid. You can put money on that."

As Race stepped to the side to use the phone I felt bad for Scarlett. Kevin and me had our shit but I knew he would never deny me while I was in the hospital after having his baby.

I was just about to brush Scarlett's red hair, which she loved, when my phone rang. I pulled it out of my pocket and was irritated the moment I saw the name 'The Pest' flash on my screen. It was Cloud. Instead of picking up the phone I texted him.

Me: I'm busy.

I waited for a few moments by pacing the small spot in Scarlett's room I was standing in. Any interactions with him took a lot out of me. And that's wild since I'd been in war before with the military.

Cloud stayed on my fucking nerves. Ever since he found out that I killed Bunny, my husband's most beloved aunt, he blackmailed me into having sex with him. I thought about killing him, or making him go missing. But he had the Band-Aid that was on my arm when I killed her. I accidently left it at the crime scene and he found it when he went to check on her. He threatened to go to the police with it since her case was now cold. If I knew where it was he wouldn't be a problem for me because he would be dead.

The worst part is outside of Scarlett; nobody else in my family knew I killed Bunny.

Cloud: Why didn't you answer the phone?
Me: Like I said I'm busy. What u want?
Cloud: Some pussy
My skin crawled and I immediately frowned.

"You aight, Bambi?" Denim asked me. "Because you look like you just seen a ghost.

I looked up at her. "I'm fine. I just saw a text I wasn't feeling that's all."

I focused back on the text and typed a response.

Me: That ain't happening.

Cloud: I guess I gotta go talk to your boy then.

My heart rate picked up and I rushed into the hallway to call him before he reached out to Kevin. I dialed his number and waited. He answered the phone after the first ring.

"Fuck is wrong with you?" I yelled without giving him a chance to say hi. "Why you always blackmailing me and shit?"

"I miss you," he said as if we were lovers. "That's why."

"Cloud, I'm not fucking around. Why you gotta play so many games? I don't love you and I never will and it be fucking me up when you mention my husband's name. I thought we had an arrangement."

"I'm not worried about your love for me no more. You just keep giving me that wet pussy and hot mouth and I'll keep your secret safe. But the moment I feel as if that has changed I'm done with you, and I'll destroy your marriage. You should've seen your husband the last time he was over here. He still fucked up about what happened to his aunt, Bambi. And I'm the only one who knows. I think you forget about that sometimes."

I leaned up against the grungy hospital wall and looked up at the ceiling. The phone was pressed firmly against my ear. "What do you think Kevin will say if he knew that I killed Bunny and you held it from him as a secret? Or that you blackmailing me for some pussy? Huh?"

"Bambi," Denim said holding Jasmine's hand. "What did you just say?

When I looked to my right I was staring at Denim. I didn't hear her come into the hallway. I was slipping. Normally I could hear someone sneaking up on me before they even thought about it.

Denim was angry. She had no idea that I killed Bunny to keep her hands off of our money and she would never understand. I could tell. In her mind family is family no matter how terrible they are. That's the main reason she took so much of her mother's shit.

I focused back on the call while looking at Denim. "I gotta go. I'll hit you later."

"Meet me at our spot in twenty minutes or else."

I hung up from him, stuffed the phone into my jean pocket and walked toward Denim. I wanted to be careful because I didn't know how much she heard.

"What's up? Scarlett okay in there?" I looked down at Jasmine who was holding onto her mother's leg. I ruffled the baby's hair a little and she smiled up at me.

"You killed Bunny?" Denim asked as a tear rolled down her face. "Did I really just hear you say that?"

My head dropped. "It wasn't like it sounded. She was trying to ruin us, Denim. I didn't want to say anything to you because I didn't want you involved. But do you remember when the boys were missing and she was coming over the house all those times?"

She nodded.

"Well she was coming over the house to take the money in me and Kevin's safe. When I wasn't looking she stole the info that we kept inside that same safe for The Russians coke delivery. She was trying to change the shipment so that it would come to her instead."

"You're not answering the question."

"Denim, she was evil! She was going to take the money and cut us out. What would we have done? Huh?"

"So you killed her for money?"

"I killed her for us. For our family." I placed my hand over my heart. "I didn't know what else to do, Denim. It was my responsibility and our husbands weren't around to help me decide."

"Does Kevin know?"

I didn't respond.

"Bambi, I can't believe you did that." She shook her head. "I can't believe you killed a member of our family. I don't know you anymore."

"You know me. I'm the one who's been in your corner from day one. I'm the one who did what I needed for this family and I would do it again. Bunny put herself in a position to be the enemy and I took her out. Is that so wrong?"

She wiped away a few tears that snuck up on her face, gripped Jasmine's hand harder and rushed down the hall.

"Denim, can we talk?" She kept walking. "Denim, please!"

CHAPTER ELEVEN

DENIM

I feel like I'm driving aimlessly down the road. Where am I going? I can't remember.

I can't believe what I overheard when I walked up on Bambi. I always knew she had her shit with her but I didn't think she'd stoop so low that she'd murder a family member. Bunny wasn't the nicest person. She wasn't even the most attractive but she was a Kennedy. And now she's gone. Although Bunny was an evil person she was still our husbands' aunt and they loved her, especially Kevin. What the fuck is wrong with Bambi?

That was always the thing that worried me the most about Bambi. In the back of my mind I knew that she could possibly hurt any one of us. As an ex-veteran in the United States military, she had the training and the skill to kill us and make sure our bodies were never found.

The fucked up part about all of this is that I want to tell Bradley so badly. He's my husband and unlike my sisters, I don't keep secrets from my man. But the other side of me would feel like I'm betraying my sister if I stepped to him about this. Since I took vows I shouldn't even be thinking about not telling him. But my marriage is different from my sisters'. Bradley and I have always had a close relationship and there is nothing I won't tell him.

There have even been times when I told my husband a close secret that one of my sisters told me in confidence and it never got back to my brothers-in-law. He was trustworthy like that and we were perfect for each other. But would he be able to handle this?

Even if he could I wouldn't want to give it to him right now with everything on his plate. He was already dealing with my dumb ass sister. The moment he broke her jaw we got back in the car and I dropped him off at a hotel out Virginia. He had plans to stay there until Grainger got well and we could be sure she wouldn't snitch.

I can't think about Bambi right now. I gotta focus on my husband and my own mess. But I did make my mind up in that moment to tell Bradley every thing. Fuck Bambi and her secrets!

My mind was going a mile a minute when I realized I didn't give Jasmine her snack. Normally she would be babbling and making all kinds of noises but I could tell she knew I was mad because she remained silent. So I reached into the glove compartment and pulled out a bag of cheese curls. I opened the bag.

"Eat these until we get home," I said placing the bag into the passenger seat. "I'll make you a sandwich later."

When I released the bag and heard it smack against the seat my eyes widened. Suddenly my heart pounded and I gripped the steering wheel tightly. I didn't want to look over at the passenger side but I knew I had to. Slowly my head moved to the right and my worst nightmare was true. My daughter was not in the car!

I screamed at the top of my lungs and made a quick U-turn. I almost hit a black Escalade and a green dump truck. With all the shit going on in my head I left my baby in the parking lot of the hospital! I've never done anything like that before.

"What the fuck is wrong with me?" I screamed. "How could I leave my own daughter?"

Dear God please keep my baby safe. I thought. *Don't let anything happen to her.*

I dipped in and out of traffic trying to think about how I left her in the first place. It didn't take me long to recall what happened.

When I found out that Bambi killed Bunny at the hospital, I rushed outside to the parking lot to get my car. Normally I would put Jasmine inside of the passenger seat and walk to the driver's side. But with the new medicine she doesn't talk as much as she usually does so I didn't sense her. She's quieter and because she's quieter I don't always know she's there. If she would've made noise like she normally did then I would've heard her.

Why didn't the stupid bitch make noise?

What am I talking about?

What's wrong with me?

I'm such a horrible mother that I'm even calling my baby out of her name when it isn't even her fault. This shit is all Bambi's fault and if something happens to my child I will never forgive her.

When I made it back to the hospital I barreled into the parking lot. I was so quick that I almost hit another car. When I made it back to the place I left my baby my body was weak.

Jasmine wasn't there!

CHAPTER TWELVE

RACE

I'm in the lobby of the hospital holding my cell phone against my ear. Denim tripping hard now! How she gonna leave her kid in the middle of the parking lot? Had it not been for us leaving early and seeing her out there, Jasmine would've walked into the middle of the street and...you know what...I don't even want to think about it. She's safe right now and that's all that matters.

When Denim doesn't respond I hang up and throw my phone back in my purse. I don't think I've been this mad in a long time.

"She ain't answer again," I told Bambi.

Jasmine is a few feet away from her kicking at the wall.

"I know Denim had the thing going on in her head with Bradley, but it ain't like her to do her kid like this," I said. "You know how overprotective she is with Jasmine. I mean really."

"You preaching to the choir," Bambi said shaking her head.

"But what is wrong with her?" I continued. I really wanted an answer and something tells me Bambi knew it. "Denim's tripping hard as fuck. I can't believe she left Jasmine in the parking lot by herself."

"If Bradley knew this shit he would flip out," she said.

I give her a serious look. "But he not gonna find out." She doesn't respond. "Right, Bambi?"

"Not from me anyway. Although I do wonder if Denim can hold secrets as good as I can."

"What's that supposed to mean?"

"Just what I said. I wonder if she can keep my secret and carry it to her grave like I'm willing to do for her."

"How you sound? She our girl. She's a lot of things but a snitch ain't one of them. Why you talking like that anyway?"

She exhaled. "No reason."

I don't know what's going on but I can tell there's a problem between them two. I'm not going to bother Bambi too much about it because right now is not the time or place. We needed to reunite Denim with Jasmine because by now I'm sure she was losing her mind.

"Hold up, where's Jasmine?" Bambi asked looking around me.

When I turned my head I didn't see her anywhere. "Oh, my God! Where did she go?"

Bambi and I hopped up and frantically looked for our niece. We went from office to office within the hospital like we had the proper authorization. Five minutes passed and we still didn't locate her.

"This can't be happening right now," I said to Bambi. Sweat poured down my face.

"It can and it is," she responded opening a door to a supply closet and walking inside. "Now the only thing we can do is find her."

A few minutes later Denim walked right up to us. She was extra sweaty and looked like she had been crying for a week. "Please tell me ya'll got Jasmine." She placed her hand over her heart and her chest moved up and down. "Please."

I looked at Bambi and she looked at me. I couldn't believe we were about to tell this girl that we had her baby but now we lost her too.

I was about to feed her the bad news when Bambi touched my hand. "I'll tell her." She looked at Denim. "Jasmine is—"

"Oh, my God ya'll do have her," she yelled looking behind us.

When I turned around, I saw Jasmine coming out of a room I know we looked in. I walked down the hall to look in the office again I figured she was probably hiding under the desk when we came inside. I closed the door and walked back over to Denim and Jasmine. I was just happy she's okay.

Denim rushed toward Jasmine, dropped to her knees and gripped her into her arms.

"Thank you, God! Thank you for bringing my baby back to me. I just thank you so much." Denim separated from Jasmine and said, "I'm so sorry, baby. I will never do you like that again."

"What were you thinking about, Denim?" Bambi asked her with an attitude. "What if a pedophile would've gotten her?"

Denim kissed Jasmine on her head stood up and stepped to Bambi. Her fists were clenched and I could see the veins pulsating under the skin on her neck. "Why would you say some shit like that? Besides, what do you think I was thinking about? Have your forgotten that quickly or do you need a reminder?"

"You better get out of my face," Bambi said slowly and calmly.

"Or what? Are you gonna do me like you did—"

Denim doesn't finish her sentence. Instead she looked at me, backed up and grabbed Jasmine's hand. Without another word she rushed out of the hospital.

"What the fuck was that about?" I asked Bambi.

Bambi ran her hand back through her long hair. "Let's go grab a drink. I need one badly."

We were at TGI Friday's restaurant during happy hour sitting at the bar. Bambi was on her fourth vodka martini and I was on my first mojito. Ever since Bambi gave up sobriety for alcohol, she pushed the limits on the bottle. She wasn't as bad as she was before drinking became a problem for her but I knew that situation was right around the corner.

"So I guess you have no intentions on telling me why you and Denim beefing?"

"I don't wanna talk about that, Race." She threw the drink back and requested another. It came right away. "And I wish you stop asking me. I heard you the first ten times."

"You going way too fast these days." I watched her wipe her mouth with the back of her hand.

"Then let me live. I got my life you got yours."

Her phone rang again, and she looked down at it. It had been going off ever since we left the hospital. I don't know why but I had a feeling she needed to get drunk to do whatever she had to when she left me, because she said she wasn't going right home.

"What's going on in your world?" She said slurring. "You always asking what's up with me, so let me return the favor. What's up with you and that mess you got going on at the house?"

I frowned. "If you mean my relationship it's not going well."

She sipped her martini. "How's that? I thought shit was moving just like you wanted. You have a man and a bitch in your bed every night even though I don't see how you do it."

"By *it* do you mean sleep with another woman?"

"Yeah, I mean where they do that at? You a married woman, Race. And you got a bitch in your bed. You can't tell me you feel comfortable with that shit. What if they get on some duet shit and cancel the trio? Fun now, heartbreak and nightmare later. I can feel it coming."

"I wish they would try and play me," I said angrily.

"I'm serious, Race. You have given him the okay to bring this chick into your home. Just be careful."

I sighed. "It's funny you're bringing this up right now. At first I was with the threesome but lately I'm starting to have second thoughts and I don't know why."

"Then why not stop it? You hold all the cards."

"Because I got feelings for both of them."

"How do you know you weren't just lonely, Race? I mean think about it for a second. You didn't bring that chick into the picture until Ramirez was gone and you thought he was dead."

"See that's what I'm trying to tell you. It ain't just happen when he went missing. Me and Ram both were fucking with that chick before he left. It's just that when he went missing me and Carey went full time. Plus every time I kiss her my pussy gets wet."

Bambi downed the rest of her drink, stood up and looked at me. "I don't like this life for you." Her phone vibrated and she looked at it, frowned and stuffed it back into her pocket. "I don't see nothing but trouble for you if you stay in that situation. And trust me, if there is one thing I know, trouble is it." She walked out of the restaurant leaving me alone.

Since Bambi had me thinking about my marriage I decided to call Ramirez to see if he wanted to get something to eat and talk about our lives. Ever since he'd been back home we'd been with Carey and there was no time to talk...just the two of us.

Part of me didn't want to have a serious conversation about our marriage because I didn't know what I wanted. Sometimes I felt like Carey was right for me and that being with Ramirez was just a consolation. Then at other times I felt I was doing what I needed to make Ramirez happy by keeping another woman around. I guess I never had a chance to be alone with myself to find out what Race needs.

I took my phone out of my pocket and called Ramirez. When he answered there was a lot of noise in the background.

"Aye, Ram."

"What's up wifey," he said. "Where you at? I been calling you all day to see if you wanted to have dinner with me later."

I smiled. It was nice to know that he wanted to be alone with me.

"I know, baby. I saw your calls. I'm sorry. With Scarlett having her baby and a few other things that went down, it's been a long day. I'm free now though. Where do you want to meet?

"Meet me at Flemings Restaurant in Baltimore. I'll wait for you at the bar until we grab a table. Hurry up though." I heard a female's giggle in the background. "Carey with me and all she keeps talking about is what plans she has for us when we get back home. Aye, Race, she got my dick rock hard just thinking about it."

CHAPTER THIRTEEN

SCARLETT

I'm lying in the hospital room watching Camp hold Master in his arms. I can't lie; it's the most beautiful thing I've ever witnessed in my life. Even when I gave birth to Samantha, my child with my first husband, I didn't feel this closeness.

"You did good, baby," he said looking over at me before focusing back on Master. "Real good. He's perfect."

"Not sure I had a lot to do with it," I admitted.

"How you sound? You carried him for nine months and he's better than I imagined." He lifted his tiny hands and then his feet. "Got all his fingers and toes too." He grinned wider. "Damn, Scarlett. He's mine. My first son."

I laughed. "You act like you didn't know I was pregnant until now."

He looked a little serious. "It's just really dawning on me. But I have no doubt that you'll be a good mother."

I thought about what he said and then my background. I wasn't so sure about that. When I was younger my parents left me with aunt Nancy Reba. She went by either her first or last name depending upon whom she was talking to.

She abused me whenever she had a chance. I have an older brother named Matt and she never did him like she did me. She would burn me, hang me over the edge of balconies and threaten to drop me. Whatever she did she wouldn't stop until I cried. She also collected voodoo dolls that she would threaten me with. When I said I would tell my parents, she would take stickpins and press them into the doll that was supposed to represent me. I felt like I was in pain even though I knew it was all in my mind. To this day I'm scared of anything involving the occult.

I was only ten years old and I couldn't understand why whenever my parents went away they took me to her house.

She did a lot of stuff to me but the thing that scared me the most was the huge silver sink in her basement. She use to fill it with cold water and ice cubes. Then she would put this step stool in front of the sink, and make me step on top of it. I begged her not to force me to do it but she never listened. She'd put my head over the sink, climb on the stool and sit on the back of my neck so that my head would stay under water. A few times she would have to revive me because I would pass out not being able to breathe.

I guess somewhere deep inside of me thinks I'll do the same thing to Master. I don't want to hurt my baby but mentally I'm not well.

"I don't want you fucking with dude no more," Camp said waking me out of my thoughts.

I felt like he gave me breath when he said that. There was nothing more I wanted to do than be with my husband. But before I got too excited I wanted to know what he meant exactly. "You talking about Ngozi?"

"You fucking with anybody else?"

"No, of course not." I sat up straight in bed and placed my red hair behind my ear. "I didn't want to be with him anyway."

"Then why do it?"

"Because I was lonely, Camp. People do dumb things out of loneliness."

Camp placed the baby down in the plastic basinet. He paced a little in the area at the foot of my bed. "Scarlett, I want to see if we can be together again. I really mean that. I mean, before I came in here I was going to tell you that I'm going to be a good father but that you and I are over. But then I looked at your face." He stepped closer. "Your beautiful face and I saw the woman I married in the beginning, before all the hurt and the pain. So I want to give it a try."

I placed my hand over my belly. "By try you mean you won't go through with the divorce?" I asked hopefully.

"What do you think?"

"But, I thought you said it was final."

"We got problems in this marriage, baby. Serious problems. Not only did we get together fast and stay together, we loved hard. Add on top of that the shit we get from people out in the streets when they see a black man with a beautiful white woman. What I'm trying to say is that this marriage ain't easy. But I'm willing to go through all of that for you."

"Where do you think we went wrong? We always loved one another but things did change. How come?"

"I think it was a lot of things. At first it was cool for us to fuck and then fight but after awhile the only thing you did was beef with me. It was like you thought that was the only way you could express yourself. Through violence."

"You did some things too, Camp."

"I know I did, and I'm not saying that I didn't. But every time I made a move you didn't like you wanted to hit me in the face. And I wanted to react but that's not in me to hit a woman."

"Well you should've hit me back."

He laughed. "You have no idea what's going on in the world do you?"

"What's that supposed to mean?"

"The moment I react physically based on something you did to me someone would see the white woman who is being abused by the black man. I can't take the risk."

"Why is everything always about race? Besides I wouldn't say anything."

"I can't believe that and even if it were true it's not the point. What's up with you and violence anyway? Why do you want me to be that way just to show you love?"

"You really think I would go to the police crying that my black husband beat me," I asked in a low voice, also avoiding his question. I did like a little violence at times. I couldn't deny it. But I would never see him get arrested. "You don't trust me."

"How could I?"

Tears fell down my face. "Camp, you married a white woman and I love you very much. Unlike some chicks I didn't go after you for your money. I knew nothing of you or your money before you stepped to me. Remember? And yes we have our shit and I can admit that, but it doesn't change the fact that my heart is for you. I wish I could get you to see that. I wish I could get you to feel it."

He walked closer to me. "You don't get me to feel it based on your words, you show me based on your actions."

"Whatever I gotta do to make it work I'm with. Just say the word, Camp."

"Okay." He paused. "I want you to tell that nigga you not seeing him no more." He walked over to our son and brushed his face with the back of his hand. "Then I want us to seek some counseling. If we gonna work we might have to get some help."

"Done!"

I had no problems telling Ngozi's ass I wasn't trying to be bothered. After what he did to me it would be my pleasure to end our little thing. Besides, if I had a chance to get back with my husband, that's what I was going to do. There's nobody in the world that could make me feel like Camp and I needed him in my life. Forever and always. I know the cards are stacked against us but that just makes me want to fight harder. I would die for him. I would kill for him and I would do anything else I could to let him know that I was in his corner.

"Is there anything else?" I said hopeful that I could make our marriage work.

"Yes. I want you to set a meeting up with him. But when you do I'm going to be there. I want to look this nigga in his eyes so he'll know to stay the fuck away from my wife. So he'll know how serious I am. "

I swallowed the lump in my throat.

I didn't see that coming.

CHAPTER FOURTEEN
SCARLETT

I was sitting in my room on the bed with the door closed. Bambi and Race are with me and I'm trying my best to explain to them what Camp wanted without losing my mind. If he meets with Ngozi I wasn't sure how things would pan out. I never knew Ngozi to be violent outside of what he did to me in the bathroom, but there was something evil about him and I couldn't put my hand on it.

"Ya'll don't understand," I said looking up at them." Ngozi not gonna take this shit easy. He once told me if he ever got the chance to meet with Camp alone that he wouldn't hesitate to kill him. I can't let them hook up, I just can't. Especially now. Me and Camp are really trying to make a go of our family."

"First off, Camp ain't no soft nigga," Bambi said. "If he's making a move like this he's probably already put shit in motion to make sure things is safe for you and him. He's a Kennedy, Scarlett and sometimes I think you forget that. So I feel the need to keep telling you. I don't know what your life was like before you were married into our family but we gangsters."

"She's right," Race responded. "You're probably worrying more about this than necessary. If you ask me Camp should've stepped to the nigga a long time ago. I'm just happy he's thinking before making a move. I guess that's what happens when you have kids."

I stood up from the bed and walked toward my dresser. I picked up my gold brush and stroked my hair. "I know we have an army. And I know we can take care of business if need be. But I think Ngozi is a different kind of killer." From the mirror I looked at Bambi and Race. I could tell I had their attention.

"What do you mean he's a different kind of killer?" Bambi asked. "If you ask me there ain't but one kind."

"His family practices voodoo. And I know for a fact that his mother has killed some people who got her wrong. And before she left the hospital after I gave birth to Master she said something in African as she stood over top of my bed. When I asked Ngozi what it was he said it was a prayer that me and him will be together until our dying day." I placed the brush down and turned around to look at them. "This shit is serious and I wish ya'll would understand that."

Bambi and Race glanced at one another before breaking out in laughter. Bambi fell out on my bed while Race dropped to the floor. They were holding their stomachs and their designer shoes were up in the air. Where was the humor because I didn't see it?

"It's not funny," I said angrily. I crossed my arms over my chest. "Stop playing around, ya'll."

"Yes it is funny, bitch," Bambi giggled. "I can't believe you getting all worked up over somebody who practices voodoo. Don't you know that shit don't work unless you believe in it? It's all in the mind."

"Nothing works unless you believe in it," Race added. "And that goes for your marriage too. The only thing you need to be doing right now is finding out what that husband of yours wants and how you can give it to him. Don't let that black mothafucka take your second chance away. Camp said he wants to work on your marriage so set the meeting up."

"You talking about marriage like you respect it." I said to her. "When you got a man and a bitch in your bed every night."

"She's right about that," Bambi said.

"The difference is I'm feeling my situation," Race responded. "It works for me. But you aren't feeling yours."

"Are you, Race?" Bambi asked. "I mean you say you like your scenario but you don't look so happy."

Race walked over to the chair in my room and sat down. "I'm not talking about me right now anyway." She looked down. "I'm talking about you." She looked up at me. "If you ask me the way you acting, Scarlett you must not want the marriage anymore. If that's the case just come out and say it."

I sighed. "I do but I am scared," I said.

"Don't say that shit again," Bambi said walking over to me. "You can't began to know what scared is unless you've seen your friend get blown up in front of you by a landmine."

She was right.

There was a light knocking outside of my bedroom door. At first I thought it was Camp with Master until I remembered he went to show the baby to some of his family members.

I got up and walked toward the door. I opened it and I saw Jasmine. She was sitting on the floor playing with a brown wooden box. When I walked in front of her she was stuffing something green in her mouth.

I looked back in my room and said, "Ya'll come here and see this shit."

Bambi and Race rushed outside of my room and we all looked at Jasmine. She was eating weed. Just as I said that Denim rushed up the steps. Bradley had just come home after being on the run and they've been held up in the room fucking. Usually Race or Bambi watched Jasmine but they were with me so the kid was left to fend for herself.

"Jasmine, what the fuck are you doing with my box?" She snatched it out of her hand and picked her up.

"She's eating your pack," Bambi said with an attitude. "That's what she doing."

Denim rolled her eyes, dug into Jasmine's mouth and pulled the weed strands out. She plucked them on the floor. Me, Race and Bambi looked at one another.

"I didn't see her get into my shit," Denim said with a look of guilt on her face. "Ever since she been on these meds she's been different. I'm sorry ya'll."

"Are you sure she's going to be okay?" Bambi asked.

"She's fine. What you need to do is focus on yourself and your own business," Denim said as she and Jasmine caught the elevator downstairs.

We all walked back into my room. "That was weird," I said to them. "She better watch that kid."

"Like you better watch yours," Bambi said giving me the eye.

"Anyway like I was telling you, Scarlett, before Denim," Race said. "You're a Pretty King, Scarlett. And we aren't supposed to scare easily. Camp will handle the Ngozi situation like he sees fit."

"Then what can I do to help him?" I asked them honestly. "I know I shouldn't be worried but I am. And to tell you the truth I'm more concerned for Camp than I am myself."

"I asked you before so I'll ask you again. What do you want us to do? It's time to decide." Bambi asked me. "Do you want him dead?"

I thought about it. Hard too. If they killed him then I wouldn't have to worry about him popping up again or him hurting Camp. My troubles would be over and I would be free to live my life with my husband and new baby. The murder game sounded good, but something in Camp's eyes told me that he wanted the opportunity to address the man who had been with his wife. If I had him killed before the meeting, he would probably think I had something to hide.

It was then that I had my answer. If I wanted things to work out between me and Camp I couldn't kill him. I had to give him the opportunity to face Ngozi. And if he wanted to give the word to have him murdered afterwards then so be it.

"I don't want him killed," I said.

"Then what do you want?" Bambi asked. "Because I'm tired of having this conversation about this dude. It's time for action."

"Maybe we can pay him to sit in the meeting with Camp quietly."

"Fuck are you talking about?" Bambi yelled. "Why should you give him more money than you already have?"

"Because I don't want him blowing up and things getting worse. I know he wants money so if we pay him maybe he'll go away with no problem."

"So you want him to act?" Race responded.

"Yes. And maybe for the right money he'll do it."

"You sound crazy," Race said. "You sure he doesn't have more on you than you telling us?"

"No. I'm just worried that's all. And I know it sounds crazy but I'm basically paying him to leave me alone. I'm paying him to hear what Camp has to say and to back out of our lives for good." I looked at both of them. "I think it will work. You know how greedy he is."

Bambi looked at me directly in the eyes. I tried to look away from her but she didn't change her stare. "We're going to pay him off but if he doesn't take the money and do his part I'm going to have him killed. You need to know that."

I agreed. The three of us were about to go cook when we heard screaming downstairs. I rushed out of my room and to the banister. I saw Denim covering her mouth while three police officer's wrestled Bradley from the living room and out of the house.

What was going on now?

CHAPTER FIFTEEN

DENIM

I'm standing in the police department with my entire family. Bambi, Race, Scarlett, Camp, Master, Ramirez and Kevin are all here. Jasmine was sitting next to me quietly in the chair. I didn't know how much I missed her babbling. I think in some ways it became my comfort because at least I knew she was alive.

I was pulling at my hair until Camp handed Master to Scarlett and walked over to me. "Don't worry," he said hugging me into his arms. "Bradley gonna be alright. We here for you and we got your back."

"Yeah, he's a soldier," Ramirez said standing next to us. "I know we gonna get past this."

When I looked over at Kevin he smiled. They were his brothers and if they said he could handle this shit then I had to believe them. Bradley did a lot of things before Bambi and us started handling the day-to-day operations of the business. They saw a lot of money and dealt in a lot of coke. But I never, ever before this time thought he could be locked up. And to think that all of this shit is because of my hating ass sister.

Camp gripped me a little tighter then released me. "I love you, sis. Bradley needs you to be strong and you will be that for him. So toughen up."

"You're right," I said softly.

I paced the floor for about fifteen more minutes before they brought my husband out from the back. He was frowning until he saw my face. When his eyes met mine it was like everything stopped. Nothing had any movement. We were all alone. The handcuffs were removed from his wrists and Bradley rushed up to me and kissed me passionately. He held on to me tightly and my body shivered. I knew I loved this man but it was hard explaining how much. He was my everything and I was willing to do all I could to keep him in my life.

When he was done kissing me he held Jasmine and kissed her on the head. Then he dapped his brothers and they gripped him into manly hugs. I could tell we were all relieved that he was getting out but knew it was a major possibility that he would go back inside if Grainger testified for the state.

When Bradley was done with his brothers he walked back over to me. "I'm so sorry that my sister did that shit to you," I said crying. "I'm so sorry, baby. If I actually thought she would snitch and tell the cops I would've talked to her beforehand. Now you gotta go to court for assault and battery and its all my fault."

He gripped my wet face into his hands and looked into my eyes. "You listen. Me getting locked up don't have shit to do with you. That bitch violated when she talked ill about my daughter and I put her in her place. I'd do it again if I had to. But what I don't want you doing is taking this shit on your heart. Grainger been jealous of what we had for the longest and now she got what she wanted. But it won't be for long.

I'm going to get a good lawyer and I'm going to beat this shit. Trust me."

I buried my head into his chest. I felt the firm beat of his heart against my nose. I breathed him in until I had to exhale to prevent from suffocating. There was nothing left to do. I knew he was hopeful and thought he was really able to get out of this charge. But I also saw the bigger picture.

He did some serious damage to her face. Grainger's mouth had to be wired and what was left of her teeth crumbled. Once they saw her hospital records he would be going down and I couldn't see that happening. If I wanted this to go away I had to make it happen and that's exactly what I intended on doing.

I was sitting at the dining room table while my mother scooped spaghetti into my plate. I was at the house I bought for her and I hated being here. My mother was already losing weight from the stomach stapling surgery that she had and she was finally looking like her former model self.

To my right was my sister—Grainger. She was wearing a smug look on her face and I wanted to knock it off. But I had to be careful. I wasn't in charge of the situation anymore. I had the money but Grainger had my husband's life in her hands. That made her queen for the day. So I had to eat my pride, all of it, and get her to drop the charges. It was the only way.

When the plates were dished up I looked at the food in front of me. I couldn't eat one bit if I wanted to my stomach was churning. If I even tried I knew I would throw up all over my plate. I hadn't eaten a bite since Bradley was arrested and then released three days ago. I couldn't enjoy the moments of having him home because in the back of my mind if Grainger showed up for court they would take him from me...away from our family. I was so busy worrying about the future that there was no time to enjoy the present.

"Grainger, did you get the money I put in your bank account the other day?" I asked under my breath while playing with my food using the fork. "I did it before I took the baby to get her hair done."

"Yeah, but I thought it would be more," She responded while sucking a strawberry shake through a straw due to her mouth being wired. I could barely understand her. "I know you got more cake than that, Denim. You have more than that in your purse right now."

My eyebrows rose. "I transferred $2,500. How much more did you need?"

"I need everything you got." She wiped the corner of her mouth with a napkin. "Besides you owe me big time." She paused. "But don't worry, you don't have to give it to me if you don't want to. Maybe I should just relax and make sure I show up for court when it's time to put Bradley away for the long ride."

I put the fork down. "Grainger, please don't do this to Bradley. I'm begging you. He's a good husband and a good father to our child. If he gets locked up for this shit he'll go down for a minute and I'd just die. Is that what you want?"

She laughed at me. "Well look at what we have here. The girl who stole my boyfriend is now begging me to give him back to her. But you know what, I'm not doing it." She positioned her straw again through the wires in her mouth. "I mean look at what the nigga done to me. If I do show up for court it will be within my rights."

"She's right," my mother said. "You're being very insensitive, Denim. That man has fucked up her mouth."

My mother sounded ridiculous. He may have broken her jaw but her teeth been fucked up since she started doing drugs. "How am I being insensitive, ma?"

"You're asking her to forgive the man who broke her heart and then hit her so hard she passed out. The least you can do is understand where she's coming from, Denim. Because whether you believe it or not, everything ain't about you."

"That's not fair, ma. Grainger and Bradley were over before I came into the picture."

"No," she yelled, "what's not fair is you coming into my house treating my daughter like she doesn't even matter. Look at her mouth, Denim. She's hurt right now and she doesn't need to be grilled by you."

I shook my head. She said her daughter. But wasn't I her child too?

"Why are you always taking her side?" I yelled stabbing the table with my fist. "Since the day I was born you always took her side. Why, mama? You might as well come out with it since it's obvious you don't care about me."

"I don't know what you're talking about."

"Yes you do. Whenever Grainger and I fight you take her side no matter what the scenario is and I'm tired of it. Yes I took him from her but she wasn't in love with him anymore. Even she told me that to my face before I ran away with him. The only thing she wanted to do was kill him. They weren't happily married or nothing like that."

"I did love him," Grainger said with tears rolling down her face. "We may have fought but I always loved him. I just didn't know how to show him."

It wasn't until that moment that I realized she actually cared about him. When Bradley and her were together they didn't have sex. They didn't talk and all they did was fight. He told me he met her at a club and liked the way she danced on the floor. The plan was to just fuck her and roll out until she brought him home and he saw me. He decided to hang around just to see what I was about and if I had somebody in my life. He must've liked what he saw because on the day the officially broke up he asked me to run away with him and I did. So he always loved me. From the first day he saw my face and we both felt it.

I placed my hand on Grainger's arm. "I'm sorry you feel that way, big sister. But I fell in love with Bradley and he fell in love with me. I did all I could do to do right by you. I bought you this house. I gave you money. Anything you want I give. All I asked is that you care for mama and not disrespect my baby when she was over here. But what you doing right now is wrong. You're about to put away a man whose only crime is loving me."

Spit rolled down the corner of her mouth. The wires made her drool. Grainger angrily wiped the tears from her face and threw the napkin in her lap. "Feed me."

"What?"

"Feed me," she said firmly.

"Grainger, what is this about?"

"If I ask you again..."

Afraid of what she would say next I lifted the cup and placed the straw in her mouth. I waited for fifteen minutes while she took mini sip after mini sip. My arm was sore but I didn't put the cup down until the entire cup was empty.

When she was done she said, "My shoulders are tense. Rub them for me."

"Grainger, I have to get home or..."

She gave me an evil look. A look that reminded me that she wasn't my drug-addicted sister. She was the boss. I was reminded that she was in control of my destiny and whether I knew it or not I needed to submit. So I stood behind her and rubbed her stiff shoulders until they softened under my fingertips. Her head rolled back and with her eyes closed she moaned. It sounded like a sexual moan and my stomach rolled.

Suddenly she opened her eyes and looked up into mine. "I don't know what I'm going to do about Bradley but I do know this. Before I am done with you you're going to feel every ounce of the pain I'm in right now. And when I'm finished. And only when I'm finished with you, will I let your beating heart go."

CHAPTER SIXTEEN

BAMBI

I was sitting on the couch in the living room with my husband. A glass of Riesling was in my hand and a glass of whiskey in a rock glass was in his. Soft music is playing in the background and it felt good just to be with Kevin without all of the fussing and fighting. I was really hopeful that tonight would remain like this. Peaceful and calm.

"You look beautiful," he said to me while running his hand over my thigh. "As usual."

"You always talking shit," I joked while sipping my wine. "You already got the pussy. You don't have to compliment me no more." I turned around so he couldn't see the scars.

"I'm serious, Bambi. I still remember the first day I laid eyes on you. When you walked past me in that airport I knew you had to be my wife. Remember? You were dressed in a pair of army fatigue pants and you looked like you were on a mission."

"I don't know what you liked about me that day. I looked a mess."

"It was everything. The way you moved. The way you held the gun to my head when you found out I was following you in another car."

I laughed. "Something must be wrong with you, Kevin. Who in their right mind would be turned on by something like that?"

"Me," he smiled. "Because everything you did that day said you belonged to me. You were a Kennedy. I had my share of women before I settled down with you but I never looked at any of them and said that's wifey material, before I met you."

I looked down at my wine glass and ran my finger over the rim. "If that's the case, and you really knew I was for you, why did you sleep with another woman and have a baby with her?"

He sat his glass on the table and rubbed his hands over his temples. "Bambi, not tonight. We were doing so good."

"If not tonight then when?" I leaned in. "Huh?" I paused and placed my glass down. "I know you been going over there to see her. I'm hip, Kevin."

"So you having me followed?"

"For more than one reason. For starters you disappeared and we thought you were dead so I need to make sure you safe. And secondly because I don't trust you sometimes."

"That's foul. You know I don't like that shit."

"Well you slipping. It could've been The Russians who were tailing you. Be glad it was me. What I want to know is what were you doing over her house?"

"I went to see my son, Bambi. You know I can't deny my kid and I never will. That ain't in me. I'm sorry I went outside of our marriage when we were beefing. I made a mistake. But he's still a Kennedy."

That hurt. Badly. "How did you meet her?"

"It's not that deep."

"Are we going to finally be honest with each other or what?" I asked looking into his eyes. "Tell me the entire story. You owe me that much."

He frowned and adjusted in his seat. "I want to talk to you but I'm not sure if you can take it."

"I'm a soldier. I can take anything."

He nodded. "When I first found out you had an alcohol problem I didn't know how to help you. Because I knew you were going through whatever you went through in the military and I felt helpless. You wouldn't let me in. The only person you talked to was Sarge. You kept telling me you didn't want to talk about it and shit like that. There's no worse feeling in the world than wanting to help your wife but not knowing how. So I...I..."

"Don't stop, Kevin," I said wiping the tears away that snuck up on me. I hated crying because it made me feel weak. "Be real with me."

"So I went out to the club one night. This chick was inside already with her friends and she kept looking at me. I was with Cloud and I just needed a release. I invited her to my table, in VIP and she kept talking about how I was the greatest nigga in DC, and how nobody's money could fuck with the Kennedy Kings. I knew it was some bullshit but if felt good at the time to hear. She was so proud to be sitting in the section with me and it showed all over her face. So I made up in my mind that I would do it just once."

"Do what, Kevin?"

"Fuck her," he said coldly. "I figured if I had sex with her once that would be it. I didn't even get a room. I pulled up behind the club and slapped a rubber on my dick. I fucked her right there and put her out. I never called her back and I always felt guilty."

My head dropped and my feelings were demolished. "If you slapped a rubber on why did she get pregnant?" I was so angry I was shivering.

"Because the rubber I used she gave me. I was too drunk to check it plus I didn't have any on me. I was married and wasn't carrying them. She must've poked a hole in it to trap a nigga. I never planned on going out of our marriage until that night. I dropped the bitch off at her house and never called her again. A few months later she found me in the club with my brothers and told me she was pregnant."

I sat in the seat like a statue. My heart was broken along with my ego. I was done for the night.

There was a knock at the door behind me and Kevin got up to answer it.

"Now is a bad time, Cloud," Kevin said when he opened the door. "Me and Bambi having a conversation."

Cloud walked in front of me and my heart tapped against the walls of my chest. He had been pressing me to spend more time with him recently and I had been pulling back. I'm sick of him. He probably showed up over here to intimidate me. To show me he had me right where he wanted me.

"This will be quick," Cloud said to Kevin while he was looking at me. "I'm coming to see if you got any old pictures of Bunny." There was a sly smirk on his face. "They opening the case again and needed more pictures so that they can post them and find out if anybody has more information on how she was murdered."

"I'm glad they not letting shit go," Kevin said. "Give me a second. I have a few pictures in our room."

"I got time," Cloud said as he licked is lips at me.

Kevin walked into the back while Cloud continued to stare me down. It seemed as if a building was hanging over my head. He wiped the tears off of my face with his rough hand.

"Get off of me," I said snatching my head back.

"That nigga still in here breaking your heart huh?"

"What do you want, Cloud?" I whispered through clenched teeth.

"You heard me. I'm working closely with the investigators in Bunny's case." He unzipped his pants. "And I need a reason not to give them the information I have about you." He pulled out his dick. "It would be a shame for the twins to graduate from college without their mother." He looked behind him where Kevin was I guess to be sure he wasn't coming.

"You can't be serious. You gonna make me do this shit right here? With my husband in the other room?"

"All I can say is that you better make it good and quick."

CHAPTER SEVENTEEN
RACE

Today was a weird day in the Kennedy Mansion. We were all sitting at the dinner table waiting for the big meeting. It was me, Ramirez, Carey, Bambi, Kevin, Denim, Bradley, Scarlett and Camp. Bambi's twins Melo and Noah were out with friends and Scarlett's baby and Jasmine were both upstairs sleep. We could hear Master's soft breaths on the baby monitor that sat on the table so we knew he was okay.

Bambi was just about to talk when there was a soft knock at the door. I hopped up. "Anybody expecting company?" I asked. Everyone shook their heads no.

I crept toward the door and grabbed the handle of my gun out of habit. I increased my height by tipping on my toes. I looked out the peephole and into a deliveryman's face.

"Who ordered something?" I asked looking at the family.

Everybody stared at Scarlett. She was so gullible when it came to money and products because she believed everything worked. She bought everything from a mesh bag that you had to place over your head to prevent you from having wrinkles to some cream that would darken your skin to give you a tanned look. None of the shit ever worked but it never stopped her from ordering things.

I signed for the package, closed the door and handed it to Scarlett. "Thank you." She sat it on the floor and I took my seat.

"Let's eat and then we can talk about the matter on the table," Bambi said. After we ate dinner Bambi got right down to it. "The Russians are too quiet."

"So let them be quiet," Ramirez said sipping his Hennessey. "They not bothering us so why should we care?" he sat back in the seat and rubbed the back of my neck.

"They have been pressing us out for months, Ram," Bambi continued. "They wanted the connect. And now all of a sudden they're quiet? Don't you think something is up with that?"

"Bambi, if they not around then we should leave it at that," Bradley said. "Even if they were up to something we can't make a move unless they do. Try not looking so hard into things. The businesses are doing well and profits are up. If you ask me you ladies are running the operation efficiently."

"But what would cause them to disappear all of a sudden?" Bambi continued. She stood up from the table and walked around it slowly. "Doesn't it seem slightly weird to you guys? I mean did they try to get the connect information from any of you and ya'll didn't tell me?"

"I haven't heard from them and you know Mitch moved from his old place in Mexico," Kevin said. "Nobody knows where he rests his head but you." He looked at Bambi. "Not even the girls. The most we have is his cell phone number." He seemed to resent her for that.

Bradley, Ramirez and Camp never said much when we held family meetings. Since they weren't at the helm of the operation they stepped all the way back. Kevin was different. He was the only one out of the Kennedy Kings who couldn't sit still. He wanted to know what was going on at all times and met regularly with me Scarlett and Denim on to find out the status of the operation. The others didn't care. They protected us, respected our grind and left us to it.

"I think it's weird but I also know we shouldn't be worrying about things we can't change," Bradley said. "Let's just make sure we got soldiers at our shops at all times and that the best man is always on the job. That's all we can do." He smiled at me. "Be easy, Bambi. You on top."

"He's right, Bambi," Carey said. "The money is coming in so shine. You a boss."

The moment she opened her mouth I held my head down. Although Carey did runs for us when we needed her, she was supposed to be pretty and silent in these meetings. For some reason, maybe it was the liquor or the fact that she ate my pussy and sucked Ram's dick every night, suddenly she felt she could speak on a topic like the Russians and this infuriated Bambi.

Bambi strutted toward Carey. "Are you talking to me, bitch?"

"What you talking about?" Carey responded. "It's a meeting so I'm giving my opinion."

"If I want to know how you suck Ramirez's dick or how you trying to steal my friend's husband then I'll call on you. Other than that fall back, slut. You haven't earned a spot at this table."

"Bambi," I yelled. "Why so hard?"

"Bambi what?" Bambi said. "This bitch walking around the house like her ass got a Kennedy name stamped on it."

Carey stood up and raised her dress. Right under the edge of her panties, on her ass cheek was a tattoo that read 'The Property of Mr. and Mrs. Kennedy'. I didn't even know about that. It was shiny with Vaseline so she must've gotten it over the weekend.

Carey dropped her dress and took a seat.

"So you think that makes you legal? Bitch, I can introduce you to a torturing that you're mind could never imagine."

"Well who gonna put you in your place?" Denim asked Bambi.

Bambi focused on Denim.

"Because she not the only one out of line now is she?" Denim continued.

Everybody rotated their head to Denim's direction.

What the fuck is going on with my family? First Bradley punches the dog shit out of Denim's sister. Then she calls the cops and has him arrested. Then Denim leaves her baby in the parking lot and we have to catch up with her to return the kid. The next thing I know Bambi is running around the house not talking to her husband based on a fight they had the other day. And for whatever reason Bambi isn't talking to Denim. I'm confused.

"Denim, if you wanna talk to me about some blood related business then we can do that in private," Bambi said. "But please...don't grandstand on me and get your feelings hurt." Bambi looked over at Jasmine. "If you know what I mean. I'm not the only one who's holding secrets."

"What you gonna do? Kill me too?" Denim asked.

Kevin looked at Denim and then his wife. He must've thought they were fighting as usual at first. "What the fuck is that supposed to mean?"

Nobody responded. Instead Bambi and Denim stared each other down and Bambi looked hurt. It was if Denim betrayed her.

"I don't know, why don't you ask your sister-in-law," Bambi responded to Kevin. "Tell him, Denim. What are you talking about? You got the stage now."

Silence.

Kevin looked at Denim. "What's going on, sis?"

Denim remained quiet.

"Denim what you talking about?" Kevin said louder.

Instead of answering Denim wiped her mouth with the napkin and got up from the table. Bradley followed her.

"Okayyyyyyyyyy," Carey said sarcastically. " This seems a little too serious for me. Let me leave too." She looked down at me and kissed my lips. Then she kissed Ramirez. "I'll be upstairs waiting to have some fun. This meeting is a downer and has killed my vibe." Carey took the elevator upstairs and out of sight.

"I don't know what the fuck is going on in this family, but I'm going to find out," Kevin said.

"There's nothing to find out," Bambi responded. "Denim got some stuff going on and she taking it out on me that's all. It's sister shit."

"You really think I'm that dumb," Kevin replied as he stood up and looked into Bambi's eyes. "I'm going to find out what's what. And it will be soon too." He walked away from the table.

"I'm going to check on Kev," Ramirez said to us.

Camp looked over at us and said, "I guess that's my queue too." He left the table.

When the fellas left, me Bambi and Scarlett were sitting at the table alone.

"What the fuck is going on around here?" I asked Scarlett and Bambi. Neither of them replied. "Somebody talk to me! What happened between you and Denim?"

Bambi looked at me and then at Scarlett. Scarlett nodded and Bambi lowered her head. I could tell whatever went down between Denim and Bambi, Scarlett knew about it already.

"You know I'm a holder of your secrets, Bambi," I said honestly. "There's no reason to think that will change based on what you tell me now. Be real with me. What happened?"

She looked up at me. "I killed aunt Bunny."

My jaw dropped and she went on to explain everything. She told me how Bunny was blackmailing her for money and how she was trying to steal the cocaine from the drop off The Russians. She talked about the fight she and Bunny got into and how she murdered her so that we would have a future. As fucked up as the murder was I believed Bambi really didn't want to commit the crime. Bambi was all about family when Bunny was anything but. If Bambi said she had to murder her that's what it is. I just wish I could've helped her dump the body.

"You know the secret is safe with me but does Denim know?" I asked Bambi.

"Yeah. She walked up on me while I was on the phone at the hospital getting blackmailed by Cloud. So I guess she's blackmailing me too."

"Now I see why you two were at each other's throats. But what the fuck is Cloud doing blackmailing you?" I asked prepared to blast a hole in his face.

"He's making me have sex with him and shit so that he won't tell Kevin. I'm telling ya'll, my skin crawls whenever he touches me. I can't take it. But what can I do? If Kevin finds out its over and I can't have that either."

"So let's kill this nigga," I yelled. "Fuck are we waiting on?"

"Keep your voice down, Race," Bambi whispered. "I wanna kill him but I can't right now. You know me. If there were a way around this I would be all over it. But he has evidence that I killed Bunny that he's hiding somewhere. He even took the necklace I took off Bunny's neck. If something happens to him he made arrangements for it to get back to Kevin. At least that's what he told me. I can't risk that."

"I hate that nigga," I responded. "He been after you for the longest. I should've known something like this would happen."

When Master started screaming on the baby monitor Scarlett sighed. "Fuck! This baby is getting on my fucking nerves already!" She pushed back in the chair. "I can't have five seconds alone without him tripping. I'll be back. I'm sick of this shit!"

Scarlett hopped up from the table and caught the elevator upstairs.

When she went inside of the doors I said, "I don't know about her and that baby."

I looked over at Bambi.

She didn't respond.

CHAPTER EIGHTEEN

SCARLETT

I walked up to my baby with anger all over me. All I wanted was to enjoy some time with the adults but Master wouldn't let me. What is it about infants and kids that rubs me the wrong way? The hate. Oh my God the hate is so amazing that I have to make constant efforts not to do the wrong thing. Not to pick him up and fling him against the wall. The weird thing is this, I don't know which reaction would be worse. If I hurt my baby, part of me will feel justified because he won't leave me alone and have a moment's rest. That alone makes me feel sick. But if I let him cry and not hurt him he'll drive me crazier, and I won't feel good.

I approached the crib. His arms and legs were outstretched and stiffened. He was a mad baby. Sweat poured down the sides of my face and my red hair clung to my neck and forehead.

I was about to go shake him up when someone said, "Scarlett."

I turned around and looked at Bambi. She smiled at me before looking at Master who was still screaming at the top of his lungs.

"Are you okay?" she continued.

I nodded. "I'm fine. Why…why you ask?"

She walked deeper into my room toward me. She smiled at me again, and walked past me toward Master. She picked him up and he simmered down immediately. She rocked him in her arms. She was great with children.

"No reason," she responded. "I was just asking how you were that's all."

"I didn't hear you come upstairs."

"I move lightly," she winked. She looked down at Master again. "He's so beautiful." She gripped his little foot. "Perfect."

I wiped the sweat off of my brow with the back of my hand. "I know. I was just thinking that."

She placed him in the bed and he went to sleep. She walked up to me. "Remember when we talked in my closet and you shared some things with me? About your past?"

I walked toward my dresser and grabbed my gold brush. "Yes, Bambi. We had this convo already."

"Tell me what we talked about, Scarlett."

I brushed my red hair slowly. "I told you that I would get some help because of my past and what happened to me as a child. I'm not a kid so stop treating me like one."

"I'm not saying that you are a kid. But I'm worried about you. You just had a baby and you could be going through that post-partum thing I heard about. So stop skipping the subject and tell me why did we talk about those things back then, Scarlett? I need to hear you say it."

"Because you knew I was pregnant and you didn't want me to abuse my baby like I did my oldest daughter."

She smiled at me again. She was so calm in that moment. So assertive. I always had respect for Bambi. In my eyes she was a warrior. But if there is one thing I hate it's somebody jumping in my business and she was pushing the limits right now.

Bambi turned around and walked over to Master. She looked down at him again. He was sleeping. She stuffed her hands into her pockets and walked back over to me.

"I don't know what happened to you as a child but you don't have to do the same thing to your baby. Look at him, Scarlett. He's yours and he's God sent. You can't realize that now because whoever was supposed to take care of you as a child failed. And you were subjected to abuse but it has to stop somewhere. Do you hear me, Scarlett? I can't let you hurt that baby. He's family. He's a Kennedy."

I looked at my face in the mirror and continued to brush my fiery red hair. Tears streamed down my cheeks because I knew she was right but I didn't know how to stop it. I never laid a hand on my baby out of hate. Not yet anyway. But I wasn't sure how much longer that would last.

"I hear you," I responded.

She walked closer and hugged me. She rocked me in her arms and I sobbed. Long and hard. I didn't realize I was in so much pain until that moment. I thought about everything good and bad in my life and I silently thanked God for my family.

When I was done she released me and I looked at myself again in the mirror. "Let's talk about something else," I suggested. I wiped the tears off my face. "Anything. I don't care what it is."

"Okay. What do you want to talk about?"

"The Russians."

The look of concern was removed off her face and replaced with rage. "What about them?"

"Do you really think they're plotting to do something to us right now?" I grabbed a tissue from the gold tissue box on the dresser to wipe my face and blow my nose.

"I don't think they are, I know they are. I'm not sure if the plan is finished but I do know one thing. They will never stop pursuing me until they get the connect information. They've tried everything to get me to talk." She looked at her reflection in the mirror. "So what do you think is left?"

I swallowed. "Your family."

"Exactly," she responded. "That's why I need you all to be careful. Be watching everything and everybody around you at all times."

She walked over to my bedroom window and looked out of it. She raised her shirt and rubbed the handle of the gun. Why was she strapped inside the house?

"We worth a lot of money," she said continuing to look out the window. "And with money comes enemies. And with enemies comes assassination attempts." She closed the blinds. "You hear what I'm saying?"

I nodded. "I hear you."

She walked over to me. "So what's up with you and Ngozi?"

"I don't know. I haven't heard anything from him since I been home. I'm worried about that shit too. I reached out to him to offer him the money to meet with Camp. He never responded. I guess he can't be bought out after all. I would've never known."

"I swear the Kennedy's got more trouble than we can hold on to," she giggled.

"Tell me about it."

"You want a drink?" she asked me.

"If you mixing."

We were about to walk out of the room until Jasmine walked up to my doorway. "This for you," she said holding some strange doll out to me.

Bambi and I both stood in the doorway with our jaws hung. She never, ever spoke.

I took it from her. Smiling the entire time. Until I saw what it was.

"What the fuck is that?" Bambi asked when she saw my expression.

I couldn't talk. My voice seemed as if it were trapped in my throat.

"What the fuck is it, Scarlett?"

I turned around and faced her. "It's a voodoo doll."

It fell out of my hand and bounced to the floor.

CHAPTER NINETEEN
KEVIN

Kevin drove down the road to his destination silently. Unlike most dope boys he didn't need a booming speaker or the conversation of a stranger to keep him occupied when he traveled. The only thing he needed when he hit the road was silence. Complete silence. Besides he was moving things around in his mind and trying to figure out how to make things work out in his life.

Kevin looked at the address on the yellow Post-It pad stuck to his dashboard. He removed it to be sure it was correct. After all, the location he was going didn't seem right for the person he was meeting.

When he pulled up in front of the store and the addresses matched he parked his Infiniti. The moment he stepped his foot onto the curb Mitch, the drug connect he'd known for years stuck his head out of the store's door. He waved Kevin over toward him.

"Hurry up, man," Mitch said. "You have to see this." Mitch disappeared back into the store and Kevin could no longer see him.

On Kevin's way inside he took a moment to take in the sign. Mr. Bernard's Antique Furniture. Was this some kind of front that he owned that Kevin didn't know about? Mitch owned a lot of businesses in the states.

Kevin shook his head and walked toward the entrance. When he got inside he stood at the doorway and moved his head from left to right looking for Mitch. He couldn't spot him anywhere.

Instead of seeing his long-term business partner he saw mounds and mounds of odd furniture. There was a slight odor of aged fabric and wood in the air but it wasn't anything he couldn't move past.

Out of nowhere from the floor Mitch raised his head up and looked over a table. All that could be seen were his eyes. He was on his hands and knees, which was why Kevin couldn't spot him at first. "Come over here, man. You have to see this table."

For as long as Kevin knew Mitch, he always had an obsession with odd tables and antique furniture. He wasn't interested in simple pieces that you would see in regular furniture stores. He adored handcrafted tables with intricate patterns and designs.

Kevin shook his head and strolled over to Mitch. "What are you about to buy now? Don't you have enough furniture in that house in Mexico?"

"Come down here," Mitch said. "I'll show you."

"I'm not about to get on my hands and knees to look at no table, man. That ain't why I'm here anyway."

He gave him a serious glare. "Just for one second."

Hoping Mitch would talk about what he wanted to discuss later, Kevin reluctantly got on his hands and knees. His three hundred dollar designer jeans were covered with dust at the knees.

"Do you see this?" Mitch asked pointing at one of the legs.

Kevin looked at it but he didn't look hard enough. "What am I supposed to be seeing?"

Mitch frowned. His white skin reddened, as he looked at Kevin as if he were crazy. "Are you not looking or is it that you could care less? Which one is it?"

Afraid he would anger the wealthy drug connect before he even started, Kevin took a harder look at the leg. When he did he saw what he was so excited about. Chiseled in the carving was a man sitting on a chair. A woman sat on his crotch and behind her back was a knife.

"I see it," Kevin said. "It's a bitch sitting on some dude holding a shank."

"But do you love it?" Mitch asked him.

"If I was into tables like you I'm sure I would." Kevin stood up and wiped his hands on the sides of his jeans. "Instead I'm into money which is the reason I wanted to meet with you."

Mitch stood up and dusted the dirt from his knees. He grabbed a handkerchief from his back pocket and wiped his hands. He looked out into the store until he spotted the owner. It was an elderly black man with a long blue-grey beard.

"I'll take it." Mitch pointed at the table.

The owner approached them and shook both of their hands. In a raspy voice he said, "This is a very expensive piece which is why it hasn't sold. I'm not sure if you can afford it. It's in the thousands."

Kevin looked down at the table and thought the suggested price range was outrageous but Mitch was insulted.

Mitch laughed and asked, "Do you see my face?"

"I don't understand," the owner replied.

"I'm asking you a clear and concise question that I expect an answer to. Do...you...see...my...face?"

"I do." he nodded.

"Because I want you to look at it carefully," Mitch said. "I want you to remember every mole, every freckle and every bump."

The man swallowed and looked at Mitch. "Okay, I did."

"Good. Because if you're ever lucky enough for me to grace you with my presence you'd better never waste my time insulting me about money or prices. It's bad for your health. Am I clear?"

"You are."

"Good. Now leave me alone and have a few of your monkeys package my table."

When the owner left Kevin focused on Mitch. "That went well."

"What do you want, Kevin?" Mitch said firmly. He wasn't in the playing mood any longer. The owner blew his vibe. "I told you I didn't want to meet about business while I was in town. But you insisted it was so important. Now what is it?"

Kevin hadn't expected him to get down to business so quickly. "Well, I wanted to talk to you about the product again."

"What's wrong with it?" Mitch looked around to see who was watching them. "As far as I can tell profits are up for the Pretty Kings. You should be celebrating not worrying."

"It's not all about the paper."

"Why isn't it?" Mitch frowned. "If it isn't about the money what should we be doing?"

"I mean, it's about the money but its...well...I don't want my wife running the operation anymore. It's for her safety more than anything. And I don't understand why you can't deal with me directly. Like old times."

"Because old times don't make money. It's all about the new."

"I understand that but—"

"I'm not going to get involved in your marital problems, Kevin," he interrupted. "Now Bambi has proven her loyalty and her dedication to me. When The Russians had her where they wanted she didn't cave. She stood tall and I respect that. Even took some slashes to the face."

"So everything we've been through and all the money we made don't matter anymore? If it weren't for me you would not have met Bambi. Remember? She's my wife but suddenly I feel like hers."

Mitch laughed. "You're so foolish to worry about minute things. Did I ever tell you about the Pitbulls In A Skirt?"

"No," he chuckled. "What the fuck is that?"

"They were a group of four women who ran Emerald City projects in Southeast Washington DC years ago. They didn't want to but they did it anyway."

"If they didn't want to run it why did they?" Kevin frowned.

"Their men asked them to help them run it and they did a good job too. The situation is similar to your situation."

"If you say so," Kevin said with a visible attitude.

"It's true. Things were going good until one of the men started dealing with another female. This angered the ladies and they decided to take over the operation, forcing their men out of it all together. In the end the men lost everything. They lost their money and eventually their lives. I'm warning you not to go down that path. Bambi is a very smart woman and she loves you but I've seen her eyes. She has the ability to at-

tack, even those she loves. Isn't that one of the reasons you fell in love with her?"

Kevin appeared frustrated. *"All I know is that I want back in."*

"Well you better find a different way to convince your woman on why it should be you instead of her. Because as far as I'm concerned as of now, there's one Kennedy running things. And her name is Bambi."

CHAPTER TWENTY

SCARLETT

I'm sitting in the supply closet of my friend's hair salon. I received a call from Ngozi while I was sitting under the hairdryer preparing to get my rollers taken out and came in here for privacy. I had been worried that Ngozi was up to something, ever since I forced him out of the hospital and he didn't call me back.

"I miss you, Scarlett. Can you honestly say that you don't miss me too?"

"I'm a married woman. You know I can't talk to you like this anymore. You really need to move on with your life."

"I'm trying. But you act as if we didn't have a past. You were married then too you know."

"Why won't you take the money? Take the money and meet with Camp and let me go on with my life."

"I can't. Just meet with me one more time, Scarlett."

"You sent a voodoo doll to my house, Ngozi. My niece picked it up and everything. What makes you think I would want to see you after that? You used something I shared with you against me and it's not right."

"That it wasn't me. It was my mother." He paused. "Anyway there's something else I want to talk to you about. Something much more important."

"What is it?"

"Are you going to meet with me or not? I'm not doing this over the phone."

I looked out ahead of me at the boxes of shampoo that sat on the floor. I was trying to say the right thing. "I can't meet with you unless Camp is there."

"That's a big mistake," he said.

When I looked at the phone I saw that he hung up.

I'm sitting in the back of a library with Bambi, Denim and Race. Bambi wanted to meet here because she didn't want to be home since our husbands were there and she couldn't find another place she trusted. At least that's what she said. We sat around a brown table and Bambi sat at the head.

"We have a lot of things to discuss tonight," Bambi started. "And I'm trusting that what's said here will stay here."

"I'm wondering something before we get started," Denim said with her arms crossed over her chest.

"What's that?" Bambi asked with a slight attitude.

"Before we have this meeting that's obviously so pressing, are you going to come clean about everything? Or just the parts that make you look good? That make you look like the hero," she looked around at all of us. "After all, the sisters have a right to know."

Bambi sighed. She looked down at her hands and then she slowly raised her head. For some reason her eyes met mine first.

"Okay, Denim. You got it."

Denim leaned back in her seat, crossed her arms over her chest and smirked.

"I killed Bunny," Bambi admitted. "But it wasn't because of what you may think. Bunny was trying to ruin us and I needed our family to be protected."

"She's right," I said trying to offer Bambi some support. "Bunny was off the chain. And I'm not saying that evil deserves to be killed. But if it did, Bunny would be first in line to get what was coming to her."

Denim's head whipped in my direction. "So you trying to tell me that you knew all along?"

"Yes." I raised my head higher. "And I stand by Bambi."

"Me too," Race said. "Even though I found out recently we all know that Bunny was a mess. You do too, Denim. Besides her always intruding in on our husband's lives, she didn't want anybody to have a life unless she said it was okay. After awhile it gets dead and old. Let's not even start with the fact that she was trying to gank us for our money. What would you have Bambi do?"

"She could've told the truth."

"But you couldn't handle it," Race continued. "You can't even handle it now. Look at how you bringing the matter to the table? Suppose we didn't know? This could've caused a riff between us. Have you ever stopped to think that it may be the reason she didn't wanna tell you?"

"So you saying I can't be trusted?" Denim asked.

"Can you?" I asked Denim. "That's something you going to have to answer for yourself."

Everyone grew quiet. When I looked at Bambi and Race I could tell we were all waiting on the right answer to come from Denim's lips. Could she or couldn't she be trusted to keep our secret?

A tear rolled out of Denim's eye and she wiped it away. "I got a bad feeling about this," she said. "A real bad feeling. If we don't tell the fellas that you killed Bunny they gonna find out from somebody else and then we all are going to be un-benefit. I got enough shit going on in my marriage now. I don't need this over my head too."

"You won't be un-benefit if we all make a pact to take this shit to our graves," Bambi responded. She got up and walked over to Denim. "I know it may look like I did this shit for money but I didn't. I promise you. I got rid of her because she threatened to hurt our family. The money was just a plus."

"It was because of that money that you were able to get even better care for Jasmine," Race reminded her.

"She's right," Bambi added. "I mean look at her now, Denim." We looked over at Jasmine who was reading a book on the floor. "She's talking. She's interacting with people more. Your baby girl is coming back and it's all because we had the coins to afford her the proper care. Hate me or love me, but I'm the reason that's possible. Now you tell me…was Bunny's life worth your baby? I gotta know."

Denim remained silent.

I didn't like it that Bambi took the responsibility of Bunny's death alone. If the truth were to ever be told they would learn that I didn't fuck with Bunny either. A few days before she was murdered she tried to blackmail me by saying she would tell the girls that I had a child outside of me and Camp's marriage if I didn't tell her the details about the million dollar Russian delivery. So I was glad Bambi killed her.

"This is just so wrong," Denim said under her breath. "If our husbands find out about this shit they won't ever forgive us. I have a loyalty to you guys, but I made a vow to my husband."

"Denim, Bambi needs our support," I said. "It's as simple as that."

Denim remained silent. "I don't wanna talk about it anymore. Why are we meeting here today?"

I didn't feel a hundred percent that she wouldn't tell Bradley about Bunny but for Bambi's case I was hoping I was wrong.

"We're meeting to discuss how to deal with Ngozi," Bambi said. She looked at me. "Him getting that doll to Jasmine was dangerous. We need to attack now."

"Do we even know how she got it yet?" I asked.

"We think it was out front. She must've opened the front door and picked it up," Bambi said. "But we have two plain clothes soldiers at the house and at her school just in case he put it in her book bag without us knowing. She's protected. But what we need to discuss here is what should we do with him." Bambi looked into my eyes. "Scarlett, I wanna hear your opinion before I rule. He violated and he has to answer for that shit."

I thought about Ngozi. I didn't want him killed because I really wanted Camp to have the opportunity to address him first.

"I would prefer if he isn't killed yet," I said. "I don't want Camp thinking I have anything else to hide."

"What is it really?" Denim asked me.

"What you talking about?"

"Isn't the real reason you're afraid to have him killed is because his mother but a hex on you and you're afraid that if you die you'll be with him until eternity?"

"That's not why!" I yelled. "My husband wants to speak to him and I'm going to give him that honor. It's funny how you think your love for Bradley is greater than the love I have for Camp."

"If you say so," Denim said sarcastically. "But if you love your husband so much, is that why you fucked another nigga before you were even sure he was dead?"

"You wrong as shit," I yelled into the quiet library.

"Am I?" Denim giggled. She looked at the rest of my sisters. "If I'm not mistaken all of you jumped onto the next dick before making sure that our husbands were actually dead. I was the only one who wanted to see his body before moving on with my life. And all I'm saying is that in this scenario it sounds like you're scared that if we kill Ngozi you will die too. It has nothing to do with Camp or your marriage. Tell me my dear, Scarlett," she said with a smile on her face. "Do you really believe in Voodoo?"

CHAPTER TWENTY ONE
DENIM

I'm sitting in a chair in a cosmetic dentist's office. Grainger is having a consultation to get some new teeth courtesy of me and all the money I was dumping in her account. Since her jaw was repaired suddenly she decided that she gave a fuck about her smile. As far as I knew she was still on drugs. Which meant she was still going to get high and ruin the new teeth she's having put in her mouth.

Ever since Bradley hit her, my life has been a living nightmare. However, it wasn't just my sister who had my mind floating. It was Bambi and my sisters-in-law too. The secret I was keeping away from my husband about knowing who killed Bunny was heavy. I didn't lie to my husband ever, yet here I was doing it for them. But through it all, there wasn't a soul alive who angered me more than Grainger.

Grainger called me all hours of the night to give her money and every time I didn't submit, she would threaten to show up in court. The deal was that if I continued to finance her habit, she would not appear as a witness for the state against Bradley. Although I hoped I could trust her because I knew she loved cash, I wasn't a hundred percent sure. Something told me this was deeper. I believe she wanted me to beg for Bradley, which I didn't do when I took him away from her.

The last time she tried her hand with me, Bradley and I were in church with Jasmine. The preacher's sermon was on the power of family. I sat in the pew so lifted and inspired that morning. I even thought about possibly making it work with my mother and sister and I prayed for a stronger family. I didn't have a plan but with some work and God's help, I was sure an answer would come my way.

And then I received Grainger's phone call while I was in service. She told me she needed me to pick something up for her that couldn't wait. She said it was from a friend of hers and it was very important. She said she couldn't go herself because she was on her way back in town with our mother.

"I need a big favor," she told me. "And you owe me one."

I remember being so angry with her for intruding on my life and my time. But what could I do? When I looked over at my husband's face in my mind it was all worth it.

So I took down the address while still in church. A few members of the congregation rolled their eyes at me as I accepted the phone call.

Later on that day, with my church clothes still on, I met her friend. And not only did her friend have a package; he wanted some money to give it to me. I ended up exchanging five hundred dollars for some heroin for my sister. My skin was hot to the touch. I was so fired up that instead of leaving it in her room like she asked, I waited four hours for her to return home.

The moment she walked into the door I was about to beat her ass until she reminded me about Bradley's case again.

She had me right where she wanted me. She took the pack from me and right when I was about to leave she made me stay and watch her get high. I don't think there are words to describe how I feel about my sister anymore.

After that night she did the same shit six more times the following week. And each time I had to exchange money to buy drugs. I could've gotten her the shit for free since that's what I did for a living. But it wasn't about that with Grainger. She wanted to see me at her command.

And now here I was, about to pay $15,000 for some new teeth that she would ruin anyway. I knew she had the money but she wanted to spend mine.

"Well your new teeth will be ready in two weeks," the dentist smiled at Grainger. "I want you to sit tight. I'm going to come back in a minute with some information you need to know before they're installed."

"Thanks," Grainger grinned. When he left she sat up on the dentist's counter and looked down at me. "Did I tell you I'm getting off heroin? I'm checking myself in and everything tomorrow."

"Good for you," I said with an attitude.

"Why you looking all crazy?" Grainger continued. "These teeth aren't just for me. They're for you too."

"And how's that?"

"Because you don't have to worry about your husband going back to jail once they're put in. With the teeth, along with any future money I require, I'm not going to testify against Bradley. So cheer up, bitch," she removed a nail file from her purse and cleaned under her nails. "You're bringing me down." A cakey dirt ball flew from under her nail and landed on my pants.

I'm enraged. It was so gross.

I wanted to be careful about how I talked to Grainger at that moment. I didn't want to say the wrong thing and spend an hour begging her not to testify against my husband if she didn't like what I said. I felt like I was walking on eggshells.

I was about to dust the dirt from her nails off of my pants when she said, "Don't do that."

I looked up at her.

"I like the dirt right there."

Frustrated, I allowed it to remain. "Grainger," I said with tears rolling down my eyes. "Are you going to testify against Bradley or not?" I paused and wiped my face. "I gotta know. This shit is driving me crazy."

"I just told you I wouldn't. How come we can't spend a little sisterly time together without all the questions? How come whenever you see me we talking about Bradley? Huh? What about me and you?"

"I want it to be a me and you. I want it so badly but I have to know if I'm gonna have a husband in a few weeks and if Jasmine is gonna have a father. Tell me, Grainger. That's why I keep asking."

"The teeth are going to be nice aren't they?" she asked skipping the subject. She hopped off of the counter and looked at her face in the mirror. "They're going to be great. You think once I put them in"— she turned around to face me— "Bradley will like them?"

"What?" I frowned. "What you talking about Bradley for?"

She stepped up to me and bent down. "Do...you... think...that...Bradley...will...like...my...new...teeth?" she asked slowly. "It's not rocket science, Denim. Either he will love them or he won't. Only you know the answer."

"Are you really asking me if my husband will like something on *your* body?"

She laughed. "You took him from me remember?" she yelled louder. "You took him from me and I never forgave you for it so technically he's ours. I'm supposed to have the life you're living, not you. You're sitting over there with five hundred dollar shoes on your feet and a fifteen thousand dollar purse on your arm. That's my life you living, bitch! Not yours!"

"Are you gonna testify against Bradley," I asked huffing and puffing. I was losing my patience quickly.

"Every time he tastes your pussy, or moves inside of your body, I'm the one he's comparing you to. Me," she yelled. "And it kills you doesn't it?"

"Are you gonna testify against my husband or not, Grainger," I repeated now less patient.

"I hate you," she continued ignoring me. "I fucking hate you for everything you've done to me!"

I held my head down. There was no use in talking to her and I finally got it. I exhaled and took in a few quick breaths. Grainger's sole purpose in life was to hurt me. It's not about her testifying against Bradley. It's about how much she can control me and how much she can make me do.

If Bradley knew she was blackmailing me to keep him out of jail he'd probably divorce me. He told me right after the incident happened that I couldn't let her see me grovel and that's exactly what I was doing.

I grabbed my Celine bag off the floor stood up and looked my sister directly into her eyes. "I'm sorry you thought I hurt you when I moved on with Bradley. I really am."

"No you're not," she pouted.

"I really mean it, Grainger," I said wiping the tears from my eyes. "I'm sorry that I created a life with a man you obviously loved. And I battle almost every day with that fact. But he's my husband now and you're going to either have to respect it or stay out of my life. You have my sympathy. But there is something you will never, ever have. And that's my husband." I looked deeper into her eyes. "Do you hear me? You will never have him. I love him too much. And if you come in the way of that I will hurt you."

Grainger cried hysterically while yelling fuck me to my face. I waited until she simmered down to restate my point. I wanted to make sure she understood.

"Do you hear me? I will murder you, my dear sister and would have no qualms about it."

I walked around her and toward the door. "Oh, and by the way, pay for your own fucking teeth. I'm done being your flunky."

CHAPTER TWENTY TWO
RACE

This gotta be the ugliest shit I have ever made and I love it. It's a mask for an independent movie company that specializes in horror films. I dipped my paintbrush into the white small cylinder on the table containing paint remover. I wiped away some of the extra black paint around the eyes on the mask. When I was done I smiled. I've created a lot of scary shit in my lifetime but this has to be my best work. It looks so real.

Ever since word had gotten around in the industry that I could make anything from full body prosthetics to real life silicone masks I get no less than fifty requests a week. From transgender men wanting silicone body molds to movie execs, I was always working. I don't need the money but it's honestly the only thing that keeps me sane.

Since I've been working on this mask for the past five days, and it's finally dry, I put it on. I walk over to the mirror in front of me and look at myself. If it wasn't for the white tank top I was wearing with my cleavage spilling out, you wouldn't know it was me.

The mask was of an African American man who had been dragged down the street on the side of his face. The left side of the mask shows pink flesh from the skin being rubbed off and one of his eyes is hanging out of the socket.

"You know you're supposed to lock this door," Ramirez said walking up behind me. He didn't see my face yet. "So we don't bother you when you're working."

"I know but I forgot," I responded wondering what he wanted. I didn't turn around right away because I decided to scare him first.

"How come I always find you down here?" Ramirez said to me.

When I turned around and he saw the mask he looked like he almost jumped out of his skin. He bumped up against the doorframe trying to get out. I took it off and laughed.

"It's just me, baby. Damn. Why you tripping?"

He held onto his heart. "What the fuck is up with you?" He breathed heavily. "How the fuck can you do this shit all day? Something must be wrong with your ass."

I put the mask on my work desk next to the cylinder. "It's my passion."

"Well as rich as you are you need to find another one. Something that doesn't make you seem so deranged."

"I'm deranged because I like to make horror masks?"

Silence.

I rolled my eyes. I guess his answer was yes. "You knew how much I loved this shit when you married me, Ram." I grabbed a towel on the desk and wiped silicone powder off my hands. "Anyway what you doing down here? You only come to the basement when you want something important." I threw the towel on the table.

"Yeah, and now I remember why I stop coming down this bitch. You keep trying to scare the shit out of me with your work." He shook his head. "Anyway, I came down here to see where you've been. I haven't seen you since you left me and Carey in bed this morning." He looked at his watch. "And now it's five o'clock pm. I've been calling you all day on your cell. Why you haven't answered the phone?"

"I been busy."

"I know that, Race. But you know I can't stay away from you too long," he said seductively.

"So what, Carey not up there no more? To keep you company?"

He stepped back and looked at me sideways. "I know you not coming at me about her like it's a problem now."

"What's that supposed to mean?"

"For starters I might have brought her into our relationship but when you thought I was dead you kept her around," he said pointing at me. "If anything I would think you'd be okay that I was still with it."

"I know. You're right."

"If you know then what's the problem?" He sat on the black leather sofa in my studio and I walked to the small refrigerator and grabbed two beers. I walked over to him and handed him one.

"I guess I'm confused." I popped the cap from my beer and took a large gulp.

"Well talk to me then, Race. This shit ain't for us."

"Are you happy with the way things are going?" I asked sitting next to him. "With me, you and Carey?"

"I'm having a good time. But I'ma tell you the truth; I'm happier when I see the smile on your face when she walks into the room than I am fucking another bitch. Or how you look into her eyes when we all make love. I can see she makes you feel good so I feel good too."

I didn't realize he was so perceptive. Whenever the three of us are together I assumed it was all about the sex.

"You are feeling her right, baby?" he asked me. "Or did I miss something?"

"I think so. But I'm so confused."

He put his beer down on the floor and reached for me. "Come sit on my lap."

"I'm not doing that shit right now, Ramirez." I took another sip of my beer. "It's dumb." I burped. "Anyway we talking about some real shit."

He frowned and seemed disappointed. "Since I've been back that's the only thing that changed about you and I'm not gonna lie, I really miss it."

"What's that?" I asked.

"You not submissive anymore, Race. Sometimes you are but it's different. Back in the day I couldn't pull you out of my lap. Now I gotta get you drunk or call on Carey just to get you to be my wife again. The one who needed me to protect her. Remember? I don't give you shit about running the drug operation because I don't care about things like that. I don't say anything when you tell me you not cooking even though I love your meals. But you do make me feel like less of a man when you don't let me hold you like I want to."

"That's not fair, Ramirez. You know you'll always be my man."

"I'm your husband, not your man. Now get over here."

He reached out for me again. I placed my beer on the floor and like he wanted I crawled into his lap and placed my nose against his neck. I inhaled deeply and could smell the cologne and soap on his skin. My pussy jumped and I shivered. He was definitely a weakness for me.

"There my baby go right there," he said softly. "I can feel your body warming up." He kissed me. "Just like I like it."

I exhaled and raised my head to look into his eyes. "Ramirez, are we doing the right thing by having her in our home? In our lives? Do you ever wonder if maybe we moved too fast?"

"Is that how you feel?"

I looked into his eyes. "Sometimes."

"Then she's gone."

My eyebrows rose. "Are you serious?"

"What's your name?"

"Race," I responded in a confused tone.

"Naw, what's your mothafuckin' full name?"

I smiled knowing where he was going with it. "Race Kennedy."

"Then let it be done."

He grabbed his phone and texted somebody. A few minutes later Carey came strolling down the stairs. He must've texted her. She wore a big smile on her pretty face and she was standing in the middle of the floor. She didn't say a word but I could tell she was ready to serve.

"Yes," she smiled with a lustful look in her eyes. "How can I help you two?"

She smelled of weed and liquor. She must've been up-stairs getting high with Denim. That was their special time together.

I looked at Ram waiting for him to answer her. This was his performance not mine so I wasn't sure where he was going with it.

"You gotta pack your shit and move back to your own crib, shawty," Ramirez said to her. "I want you gone today. Don't let the nighttime catch you."

144

Her jaw dropped and tears rolled down her eyes. I leaned in because I hadn't expected him to go so hard. He acted like he didn't even know her. Like she was a bum broad off the street. I felt badly for Carey.

I'm a thorough bitch but it was difficult for me to look at her so I turned my head. Instead I focused on the mask I'd taken off moments earlier sitting on the table. It was way prettier than this scene right now.

Carey started sobbing. I think she was talking too but I didn't understand what she was saying.

"Come here," Ramirez said to her in a cool and calm manner. He reminded me of one of them 1970's pimps.

Carey dropped to her knees right where we sat. We looked down on her as if we were playing God with her life. Maybe we were.

"What did I do?" she cried. "Tell me. Is it because I was beefing with Bambi? During the meeting?"

"Stop crying," he said softly. "Now I'm feeling you, we both are, but this is my wife. And we've been moving so fast that we haven't had a chance to see who we are without you in the picture."

Carey looked at me and touched my hand. "Race, aren't you happy with me anymore? If you not what can I do to apologize?" she wiped the tears away. "And prove how much I love you. I'm willing to do anything."

I looked into her eyes. At one point I was her rock. I was her soldier. I provided everything she needed. And now here I am, sitting in my husband's lap feeling weak. I'm starting to wonder if this wasn't what Ramirez wanted all along. Maybe the plan was always to give me too much of a fun thing so that my attention could be back on my marriage. If it was his plan, it definitely worked.

I looked down at her. "You heard my husband. It's time for you to bounce."

CHAPTER TWENTY THREE

BAMBI

I'm in Tyson's Corner, a luxurious shopping mall in Virginia buying my twin boys anything they want. Although they usually went shopping on their own, this time I told them I wanted to be there to make sure they bought everything they desired for college. Truthfully I just wanted to spend quality time with them.

Ever since Bunny sent her friend Therese to send that letter to Melo and Noah, Noah had been giving me the blues. The letter implicated me in Bunny's death if something happened to her. Noah hated me for it and he never forgave me, even though I lied and said I wasn't involved. If it wasn't for Melo's love and grace I think I'd be a wreck now.

Add to that shit that Kevin has been acting funny lately. I don't know if he's closing in on me being the one who killed his aunt or if he's still salty that Mitch doesn't wanna do business with him directly. Whatever his thing is he was taking it out on me and it's weird. I can't remember the last time we fucked, and it use to be every day. Sometimes I wondered if the scars I wore on my face changed his mind about me.

"Okay, boys, since you got everything you wanted what do you say we grab something to eat before we go home," I said to them at the Gucci counter where they just hit me up for $6,500.

"If the gospel be told, I really want to go home," Noah said with an attitude. I hated when he said that gospel shit. "I got plans tonight."

"So you had time for me to spend some paper on you but no time for quality?"

He laughed. "Come on, ma. You and me both know money ain't a thing in this family. I mean ain't that why you threw us in a boarding school? So don't act like you looking out. It's pennies to you."

Embarrassed I looked over at the cashier who looked away. "How come whenever I wanna spend time with you, you hit me with that gospel shit?" I asked Noah. "Yes, I know money is available but it's not easy either. I work hard for this shit. And if you truthfully understood gospel you'd know that it's wrong how you treating your mother."

"I wonder what the gospel says about aunts? Since that letter aunt Theresa gave us said you had something to do with killing aunt Bunny," he responded.

"Don't say that," Melo told his brother. "We out in public."

"It's okay, son," I said to Melo who was always upset at how his twin brother treated me. I looked at Noah. "If you really think I had something to do with killing aunt Bunny why didn't you tell your father?"

"Because it would kill him. And unlike what I feel about you, I love my father more than that."

Noah tried to give Melo some dap but Melo wouldn't accept. He was always on my side.

"Fuck it then," Noah said. "You stay sucking on mom's tits like you a baby. I'll catch ya'll back at the crib."

Noah left and two of the four armed men, I had with me, followed him out the door. Because I didn't know what was going on with The Russians, I had protection on my sons at all times. Even when they had sex with these little girls, although they didn't know it.

The other two armed men with me grabbed our packages while Melo and I stepped outside of the shop.

"What about you?" I asked Melo. "Are you willing to have lunch with your mother?"

"Anytime," he said in a way that melted my heart. "You already know that."

We ended up at Swards Seafood restaurant in Virginia. It seemed like time floated by whenever he and I were alone. We laughed and joked and had a good time and it made me feel so special. Say what you want about Melo, if there was one thing I knew it was that he loved his mother.

"Melo, how come you love me so much?" I asked sipping my martini.

"Because you're perfect to me." He looked at my drink. "Well, outside of the drinking shit." He sighed. "I wish you hadn't started that again, ma. You were doing so well and I wasn't worried about you as much."

"You don't understand. This is a release for me. If I didn't have a little here and there I think I'd be dead by now."

"And that's what I'm afraid of."

He touched my hand. The one that was holding the stem to the martini so I placed my drink down on the table.

"It's going to get bad and you're going to be an alcoholic again," he said. "I don't know when but it will. You gotta catch it now."

"You sound so old."

"I'm serious. I love you, mama. I think you're beautiful, sexy and fun. And if I was going to have a wife I would want her to be just like you."

"But why?" I blushed.

"Because you're my idea of a strong black woman but you don't know it anymore. As tough as you are, I see you're still fighting to find out who you are and what you want out of life."

"Melo, stop."

I held my head down and he lifted my chin.

"No way," he said firmly. "I don't want you holding your head down. Not when your prince is in the room and he needs your love."

I looked at him and smiled. "I don't know where I went wrong with Noah but I thank God for you everyday."

"Thank him for both of us. Ma, Noah's just hurt that's all. He had an expectation of how he wanted you to be and for a second you didn't meet it. But I see the strength in you even if you're drinking. I adore you and he does too. I bet you if something happened to you he'd lose it because of how he's treating you."

I exhaled. And then I tightened up. I wiped the corners of my mouth with the white cloth napkin in my lap and stood up. "I'll be back, son. I'm going to the restroom."

He winked. "I'll be waiting."

My security team motioned to follow me, but I waved them off to stay with Melo. Instead of going to the bathroom I kept walking straight ahead. I didn't stop until I was outside of the restaurant and sitting in between Iakov and Arkadi Lenin— The Russians. Our arch nemeses. We were on a bench.

"When are you going to tell me how you do that?" Iakov said holding a clear cup. I'm sure it's vodka like always.

I cross my legs. "How do I do what?"

"What my brother wants to know is," Arkadi said. "How do you know when we are watching you?"

I smiled at them both even though I was seething mad. How dare they come so close to my sons and me.

"Well if I told you that I'd have to kill you." I paused. "Both of you. Now what do you want? I have things to do." I stared into both of their piercing blue eyes. I wanted them to know that I was deathly serious.

Arkadi laughed but Iakov did not.

"After we did the artwork to your face, you made a promise to us," Arkadi said. "Do you remember that promise?"

I nodded. "Yes."

"What was it?"

"I said I remember."

"What the fuck was it?" he yelled.

I looked around at a few people walking by. We probably looked strange on the bench. Me, the black woman with the scarred face sitting between two white men with blue eyes.

"I said if you let me go I would consider giving you the connect information in about a year."

I hated the promise I made to them. But it was the only way they would let me go without castrating me. The sad part is I have no intentions on handing it over because it was the only thing that was keeping us alive.

"No, you promised us you'd give us the info if we left you and your family alone for a year," Iakov said. "We've done that."

"I thought about it," I said trying to remain calm even though my heart kicked wildly inside of my chest. "I'm not going to be able to give you the information. I don't understand why it's so important to you anyway. I'm still supplying you with quality coke at a great price."

Iakov sipped the rest of his drink and sat it on the ground. He looked over at me and said, "You know something? Even with the marks we put on your face you're still beautiful."

"That's because beauty is in the mind and heart," I told him.

He nodded. "You have no idea who you're fucking with right now do you? You are under the impression that we're one of them nigger soldiers on the street. If you do think that you need to understand that we aren't, my dear Bambi. We are the monsters in your president's dreams. We are the real terrorists of the USA. And we have the ability to put this entire nation to sleep."

"All of that for some cocaine?" I joked.

They were silent for a minute before bursting out in laughter.

"Look inside of the restaurant, my dear Bambi," Iakov said. "I wonder if you'd find what we see so amusing."

I followed his orders. I saw a waiter giving my son water. But when the waiter lifted the back of his long sleeve white shirt, I saw the butt of a gun. My heart stopped. The waiter released his shirt and continued to serve my son.

"Don't make us annihilate your entire family," Iakov said in a loving tone. "I don't want to do that but I will. Give us what we want, or we will put your precious twins to sleep."

"Permanently," Arkadi added.

CHAPTER TWENTY FOUR
SCARLETT

I lied to Ngozi and told him I would meet him alone because Camp kept putting the pressure on me about the meeting. I had Bambi and my sisters put $100,000 in the trunk of his car while he sat in the meeting. I hated deceiving Ngozi but he wouldn't meet with Camp any other way. I hope this wouldn't bite me in the ass later.

So now I'm in an empty conference room with Ngozi and Camp. Eight armed men covered us. Camp paid a dude five hundred dollars for one hour to rent it. The room seemed too big for the purpose and it made me a little uncomfortable.

"I appreciate you coming," I said to Ngozi who had a flat expression on his face. "I know you didn't have to be here so thank you."

Ngozi didn't respond. Instead he eyed my husband. His stare was intense.

"My wife is beating around the bush but I'm not gonna be as hospitable," Camp said. "I want you to stay away from my family. Effective immediately." He paused. "When I was gone my wife did what she felt she needed to in order to get over me and she chose you. But I'm back now and I don't want you around anymore."

Ngozi nodded. "Okay," he said flatly.

And then he stood up and walked toward the door. Before leaving out he turned around and said something in African that as usual I didn't understand. Although I had no idea what he said my heart stopped.

Ngozi smiled, opened the door, and walked out.

"I guess that's settled," Camp said looking at me, before nodding at the armed men.

"I guess you're right," I responded not believing him.

Ngozi left too easily. Something doesn't feel right. I don't know what was on his mind but I do know this. Leaving me alone was the last thing Ngozi intended on doing.

CHAPTER TWENTY FIVE
DENIM

I woke up with Bradley's dick stuffed deeply inside of me. I was lying on my back and he was on top of me looking into my eyes. Whenever we made love he did that and it drove me crazy. Sex with him was so passionate and slow. He took his time with me and it was as if it were the first time, every time.

He maneuvered his body to the right and softly sucked my nipples as he continued to fuck me. My body tingled everywhere and I couldn't help but get wetter. His breaths became so heavy I thought he would hyperventilate. If I knew one thing it was that my husband loved everything about me and that included sex.

I could feel myself about to cum and I bit down on my bottom lip. He raised his head and started sucking on my earlobe as he continued to stuff me with his hard dick. I was in ecstasy.

"I love you, Denim," he said taking a moment to look into my eyes while my pussy drenched his rod. "I would give my life for you. And no matter what, I don't want you to ever forget that."

I knew he was holding back on the orgasm so that I could get mine and that made me love him even more. He always did what he could for me even in the bedroom. I'd rather die and leave everybody behind if it meant I could keep my husband. I know it's wrong but that's the type of relationship we have. I feel like I'm not complete without him so what kind of mother would that make me if he wasn't in my life? This is the main reason I need him to stay out of jail. The sanity of my family depended on it.

I was just about to cum until there was a small knock on the bottom of the door. I tried to ignore it and Bradley did too. I could tell because he continued to stroke inside of my wet pussy like nothing was happening even though his body stiffened when we first heard the knock. But then the knock grew louder and there was no denying the distraction.

"Who is it?" I yelled while my husband buried himself deeper inside of my pussy.

Nobody answered so I continued to give him full reign over my body. But the sound grew louder.

"Who the fuck is it? I'm not playing!"

"Mommy," the voice said.

Shit! It was our daughter. Ever since she'd been taking the new medicine she knew one word above all. Mommy. She use it for everything too. If she wanted potato chips she'd say mommy. If she wanted to go to the bathroom she'd say mommy. If she wanted strawberry ice cream, she asked if she could have some mommy.

I love my daughter, I swear I do but I need this moment alone with Bradley. Besides, our time together wasn't promised anymore.

My sister was angry because I cut her off the payroll and I was sure she was actively trying to find ways to get her revenge. But Bradley said he didn't give a fuck. When I told him how she had been treating me, he told me not to kiss that bitch's ass anymore, even if it meant he had to go back to jail. He said give him his dignity or give him death. And I decided that I would ride with him on that note no matter what.

"Tell her to come back, Wet Wet," he said kissing my neck.

"Wait a minute, Jasmine," I said trying to hide the tingling sensation taking over my body. "Come back later!"

The knocking stopped and suddenly we were alone.

"You sure I should be telling her to come back?" I asked him as he moved slowly. "I don't want her upset."

"She'll be okay for five minutes but I needed this like yesterday," he said. "This is the first time we had sex in days."

"Just do your thing and quick before she comes back."

"We get the worst parents of the year award," he laughed. And then he looked into my eyes and smiled. "Five minutes of neglect don't mean we don't love our kid."

"So let's make this time count," I responded.

In that moment Bradley fucked me as if my life depended on this. We never, ever, in all of her life denied Jasmine when she wanted our attention. But this time it wasn't about her. It was about him and me and I loved every minute of it.

And then I smelled something strange. Something strong and serious.

"You smell that shit?" Bradley asked as smoke crept under the door.

I coughed a few times too. "Yeah. What the fuck is that?"

When I looked under the door all I saw was smoke crawling into our room. Something was on fire.

I was covered in thick gray smoke as I moved into the rest of the house. I didn't know what was burning and I didn't care. The only thing on my mind was finding my daughter and making sure she was safe. I said some hateful things about not needing my baby girl in the past. It was during my most frustrated times with her condition. God, please don't take her from me. I didn't mean it.

"Denim, I can't see you," Bradley called from behind me. He coughed a few times. "Move toward the door and I'll go find Jasmine."

"I'm not leaving without my child."

"And I'm telling you I'll find her," he yelled louder. "But I want you to get out of here. Now."

"Jasmine," I yelled ignoring him. "Jasmine if you can hear mommy come to me. Come to my voice, baby."

Normally I obeyed my husband but at the moment I wasn't paying him any mind. I sent my daughter away so I could bust a nut and now I was risking losing her forever.

My eyes burned terribly. Since I couldn't see anyway, I closed them and stretched my arms out to lead the way. But then my throat felt so dry I thought it would close up. I bumped into something hard that sat on the floor. A throbbing pain circulated through my shin but I didn't care. I reached my arm out and touched what was in front of me to go around it and that's when I felt immediate nausea. Suddenly I was lightheaded.

Where is my baby?

Where is my....

CHAPTER TWENTY SIX
RACE

My eyes are partially open and I'm surrounded in a thick gray haze. My nose and eyes burn and I feel like I'm in a sauna. Although I'm not walking I'm still moving. But it's like I'm levitating. My arms hung at my sides and my legs dangled up under me. When I raised my head a little I saw my husband Ramirez carrying me in his arms as if I were a helpless child. What's happening? One minute I was in bed sleep and the next I was... Am I dying? Am I in hell?

I tried to speak but my voice was trapped within the walls of my throat. Suddenly there was a brisk cool air caressing my body. And the red silk nightgown I wore now felt like a sheet of ice against my breasts. We were outside of the house.

When I opened my eyes wider I could see a sea of red, white and blue lights. The sirens were blasting loudly and I was forcefully snatched from my husband's arms and taken by a huge man in a blue uniform. His hands were rough and he smelled of dirt and grime, something like a car mechanic. He was a firefighter.

I was quickly placed on a bed where a paramedic looked down at me with sorry eyes. "Are you okay, ma'am?" he asked me.

I didn't respond. Instead a single tear fell down my face. What was going on?

The paramedic, with the help of another pushed me inside of the ambulance. An oxygen mask was placed on my nose and mouth and the doors to the truck slammed shut. Through the small windows I could see my house going up in flames. The Kennedy mansion was no more.

When I was about to drift off to sleep the doors flew open. Ramirez looked down at me as if he thought he lost me. "I'm going with her," Ramirez said stepping into the truck without an invitation. He was two shades darker because he was covered in black soot.

"Who are you?" the paramedic asked him.

"I'm Mr. Ramirez Kennedy and this is my wife," he said seriously. "And if you try to put me out you gonna be laying next to her on the floor."

The paramedic didn't fight him. Instead he continued to check my vitals. All I wanted him to do was get off of me.

Ramirez gripped my hand into his. His fingers were cold and his tears poured out of his eyes and fell onto my oxygen mask. I always knew he loved me but in that moment there was no denying where his heart lied.

I raised the oxygen mask slightly and asked, "Baby, what happened? Why is the house on fire?"

"I don't know." He looked back at the house as we drove away with the sirens blaring. "I'm just glad you alright. I thought you were gone. Fuck! I lost my mind."

"Is anybody hurt?"

He looked away from me and it caused my heart to speed up. Why wouldn't he answer my question? Was somebody hurt or not?"

"You need to relax, Mrs. Kennedy," the paramedic interrupted. "We don't want anything getting you more upset right now. You inhaled a lot of smoke and almost lost your life."

I looked up into the paramedic's eyes. "I want to know what the fuck happened in my house! Don't tell me not to get excited." I looked at my husband. "Baby, please tell me what happened. Are my sisters okay?"

"Yes, they all got out fine."

I exhaled. "Good. Now what about your brothers? Are they fine too?"

"Yes."

"Then who was hurt?"

I thought about Carey. She hadn't been over the house since we cut her off so I knew it couldn't be her.

"Jasmine," he said in a low voice. "She died in the fire."

I screamed.

CHAPTER TWENTY SEVEN

SCARLETT

I'm sitting in the second row of the funeral home looking at a tiny casket in the front. It's pink and has small blue hearts all around it. They were Jasmine's favorite colors. In all of its beauty it's actually the most awful thing I've ever seen in my life. I don't think any mother should have to bury their child and yet here I am supporting my sister Denim while she does it.

Denim is sitting in the row in front of me. Her blue dreads are pulled back in a ponytail holder. She's wearing black sunshades almost the size of her face and I can see chains of tears rolling down her cheeks. Bradley is sitting to her left and he's rubbing her arm while her head rests on his shoulder.

While I look at Denim's baby's casket, Master coos in my arms. I guess I should be grateful that although she is without child, I still have mine. But I'm not. Every now and again Denim would look back at me and then the baby and I can't imagine the pain she must feel right now. To know that while I just gave birth, she was now burying her only child.

When I heard loud sobbing in the back of the church I turned around. Coming down the aisle was Sarah, Denim's mother along with Grainger. Although this was a dark day they both looked fashionable in their Christian Louboutin high heel shoes and designer label dresses. It was as if they were dressed for a fashion show instead of a funeral.

Sarah looked really good due to all of the weight she'd lost from the stomach stapling surgery. And Grainger looked like she had made a come up too. I wondered how they got the money, but now was not the time to be thinking about or asking that question.

"Oh my God," Sarah screamed coming down the aisle as Grainger held her up. "Please Lord why did you take my grandbaby? Why did you take her from me when you know how much she means to me? Oh Lord, pull me out of here and take me to Heaven. Pull me out of this world and this misery because I'm not going to be able to make it!"

She was growing louder and making an awkward scene. Denim on the other hand, didn't even turn around in her mother's direction.

Bambi and Race stood up but before they could make a move my husband along with Kevin, Bradley and Ramirez were already on top of both of them. Camp stood on the right of Sarah while Ramirez stood on her left. Bradley stood in front of Grainger and I wondered if it was the first time he'd seen her since he broke her jaw.

Kevin walked up in front of Sarah. The entire church was on pause wondering what he was about to do. Instead of knocking her out he gripped Sarah's arm and whispered something harshly in her ear. I don't know what was said, but Sarah and Grainger quickly pulled themselves together and sat down for the rest of the funeral. Nobody heard much from them after that. I guess they were able to compose themselves after all.

After the show they put on, the preacher got up and said a few words for Jasmine. At this point Denim started sobbing heavily. Bradley pulled her closer so that her head could rest on his shoulder again. He kissed her softly on the cheek. My heart poured out to Denim and Bradley.

"Why God?" Denim asked standing up. "Why would you take my baby? I'm nothing without my baby." She raised her clenched fists and swung at the air. "Why? Why me?" she screamed.

I handed Master to Camp and I rushed to help my sister. Bambi and Race were right along with me. We tried to hold her in our arms but Denim was inconsolable. She dropped to her knees and before I knew it she passed out.

I was sitting in the repast with my family but without Denim. She was taken out of the funeral in an ambulance after passing out and Bradley was right at her side. At the hospital although she begged the doctor to discharge her for the burial, he wouldn't. He said that if she didn't calm down he would commit her into an institution instead and he couldn't promise when she would be released. It was hard leaving her there but we didn't have a choice. It seemed like things were getting worse for Denim. We had our problems in the past but I felt bad for her. I love her so much.

Master was in my arms fast asleep and I was happy for the break. The way my mind was going I didn't have the mental energy to soothe his whiny moods *and* be fake for all of the people who really wanted to know one thing— who started the fire?

When my phone vibrated again for the twentieth time I pulled it out of my purse. When I saw it was a text message from Ngozi my heart rocked. I hadn't heard from him in awhile and I hoped it would stay that way. Besides I paid him off and I thought things were cool. So what was happening?

Ngozi: Come outside.

I ignored the message.

Ngozi: Now.

My head spun from left to right. Where was he? It wasn't like he was invited to the funeral so why was he saying come outside?

I looked over at Camp who was talking to Ramirez. I felt safe even though I probably should not. I took a deep breath and replied.

Me: Leave me alone. Just move on with your life.

Ngozi: Don't make me hurt you. Come outside now. Besides, we have something major to discuss.

This was a nightmare. In the back of my mind I knew he had something to do with the fire but now he was confirming it. He was basically telling me that if I didn't give him what he wanted that he would hurt my family again. If this got out my sisters and my husband would never forgive me.

I had to see him. If I hurried maybe I could talk some sense into him so that he wouldn't do anything crazy again. So I tossed my cell phone into my purse and stood up.

I slowly walked the baby over to Camp and said, "You mind holding Master for a little while? I have to go to the bathroom."

He looked me in my eyes and gave me a small smile. Although it wasn't big I knew he wanted me to know that he loved me and I can't lie, it felt good."I got him, baby," he said. "Go do your thing."

After handing him our child I walked slowly toward the exit. I looked back once to make sure Camp wasn't watching and he wasn't. So I exited the room and pushed through the double doors before bending the corner. And there he was standing across the street in all white. An eerie smile rested on his face as he waved me over.

I walked at a leisurely pace toward him. I started to run back inside but I needed to get this over with. It was time to be brave. If he was going to hurt anybody else I wanted it to be me, and not my family. When I finally got up to him he removed his smile.

"What do you want with me, Ngozi? I gave you the money after you met with Camp. Didn't I?"

"I want something else."

"Then what the fuck is it?" I screamed. I looked behind me at a few people who were exiting the repast.

He grinned. "I see you're feisty now."

"I don't have time for games."

"Me either. Which is why I'm going to be in touch with you in a few days. And when I do I want you to be ready to do anything I ask."

"And if I don't?" I questioned while shivering.

He rubbed my face in the same position my husband had earlier. "You already know what I'm capable of. Haven't I showed you enough?"

CHAPTER TWENTY EIGHT
BAMBI

Since our home was destroyed we were at the large cottage house we bought in Maryland last year. Although it was called a cottage it actually had seven bedrooms, a full basement and a livable attic. The back of our home overlooked a large lake. It wasn't as glamorous as the mansion but it was cozy and warm, especially during the holidays.

I was sitting in the dining room with Scarlett, Race, Bradley, Kevin, Camp and Ramirez. Noah and Melo were there too. Denim was in the room sleeping because she was on heavy antidepressants.

We were having a long overdue family meeting, which was necessary even though I always hated them. This one was important for more than one reason. Outside of the fact that a lot of things were happening to us, it was also the first one we held since Denim lost Jasmine two weeks ago.

"I know I normally run the meetings," I said under my breath. I looked over at Kevin. "But this time I'm going to turn it over to my husband." I took my seat.

Kevin stood up, rubbed my shoulder and smiled down at me. He had a smug look on his face and I didn't want to read into it the wrong way. But it looked like he was happy I was bowing down to him. But what else could I believe?

"As you all know we suffered a major attack on our family a few weeks earlier. This attack must be answered but first we have to play smart."

"How do we play smart, Dad?" Noah asked. "We lost little Jasmine in a fire. If you ask me now is the time to fight, not be weak and smart."

"Fight who?" Melo asked with an attitude. "You always so quick to pull the trigger but you never know who you shooting."

"He's right, son," Kevin said. "I miss Jasmine too. Nobody misses her more than her father and mother, but we can't make stupid moves based on our emotions. Everything we do from here on out has to be calculated. If we jump out there without a plan we can suffer another loss."

Noah frowned and sat back in his seat. He folded his arms over his chest. "So who did this shit?"

"The Russians of course," Scarlett yelled out. She seemed nervous. "Who else would it be?"

I thought about Ngozi but he would be a fool to make a move like this on us. Besides, the last meeting I had with The Russians led me to believe that they were capable of such an atrocity.

Even though they pulled me up when I was shopping with Noah and Melo I never let my family know because I didn't want them worrying. I kept the secret and now I was wondering if it was a bad move. Was I responsible for the baby's death?

"I'm not sure if it's The Russians," I said looking over at her. "They haven't said anything yet," I lied. "And to burn down the house without asking for a price doesn't make any sense."

"She's right," Kevin replied. "The fire department said they found an accelerant all over the house. Whoever did this shit had time to come inside. The Russians are resourceful but not that resourceful. They could've never gotten past the security we bumped up recently. Chances are it's somebody we know." He looked around at everyone. Even me.

"Right and since somebody is always home it doesn't make sense that it would be The Russians," Camp replied. "Something else is going on here."

Scarlett moved uneasily in her seat.

"So what are we going to do?" Denim asked standing in the doorway of the dining room. "Sit here and talk all day or make a move?"

She was wearing a fluffy purple nightgown, which was tied tightly around her waist. Her dreads were all over her head and tearstains were dried on her face. To make matters worse from where I sat I could smell the scent of her pussy. It stank like pickled sausage and eggs.

I felt bad for my girl. Although I knew she was going through the worst scenario a mother should ever have to go through I hoped she'd pull herself together soon and be able to do small things like bathing, because right now I was worried. She didn't care how she looked or smelled and I couldn't imagine how Bradley was going through it.

"Baby, go back to bed," Bradley said in a soft tone. "I don't want you having to worry about this. We got it. I'm here so I represent you."

"Fuck the bed, Bradley," she screamed at him with clenched fists. She walked into the dining room and slowly circled the table. "None of you...not a one...knows what it feels like to lose a daughter. But I do."

"I didn't just lose my daughter too?" Bradley asked.

"You made me turn her away," she yelled. "Remember? You made me tell her to get away from the door just so we could fuck. And now look! She's gone."

"That's not fair," he roared.

"Fuck fair," she screamed louder. "Now I want the mothafuckas responsible for this shit to die, and I want it to be a slow death. None of that put a bullet to his head and pull the trigger shit. I want him to pay for everything he did to me and everything he took from me." She sobbed. "I can't believe I lost her. I can't believe she's gone."

"Baby, that's what we're trying to do," Bradley said standing up. "Instead of moving on somebody who didn't have nothing to do with this shit, we trying to play it safe and smart."

"I know who was involved," she responded before looking over at Scarlett. "Don't I, Scarlett?"

It seemed like Denim was all over the place. She was blaming everybody and everything.

"I don't know what you're talking about," Scarlett replied.

"Yes you do, bitch. You hated my baby from the first day you saw her face. And you finally were able to kill her. You poured some shit all through the house and you killed her!"

Large tears poured out of Scarlett's eyes and her face reddened. If I didn't know it before I knew at that moment that she was blame free. Scarlett would never do something like this.

"Denim, we were all in that house the night it burned down," I said seriously. I know she was hurting but throwing lies like that around could get somebody killed. "Master was in his bed sleep and he could've died too. We all could have."

"Why are you always taking up for this bitch?" she asked me. "Huh? You and me both know she could care less about Jasmine. And now she sitting over there like she's the queen with her baby while my baby's gone. She did this to me! Didn't you?"

Denim rushed over toward Scarlett's end of the table like she was about to hit her. Scarlett got up like she was prepared for anything including fighting. Denim raised her right hand and smacked Scarlett in the face so hard a red hand imprint popped up on her skin. But instead of Scarlett fighting her back she gripped Denim into her arms and hugged her.

Denim tried to wiggle away from her embrace but Scarlett must've had a death grip on her because she couldn't get away.

Finally Denim's body seemed to weaken and she wasn't fighting as much. "I miss my baby," Denim cried in Scarlett's arms. "I miss my fucking baby so much."

"I know you do," Scarlett said holding her tighter as she cried too. "And I'm so sorry, but I'm here for you. You can take it out on me. I can handle it."

"I don't think I'm going to be able to live without her. How do I live without my child?"

We all got up and moved to support Denim. The pain surrounding our family at the moment was the heaviest that it had ever been.

I'm not sure but I got a feeling that the only thing that can get us out of this is blood.

CHAPTER TWENTY NINE

RACE

After the month I was having I couldn't wait to get back to my hobby but first I had to fix up my new studio inside of the cottage. I was dumping some old movie props out back of our home.

While emptying the trash I was thinking about my family. Denim was taking Jasmine's death hard but I'm not sure what I expected. What I didn't see coming was how hard it would come down on me. I cried almost every night and I wasn't the only one. I heard Scarlett sobbing in the bathroom downstairs and Bambi had been drinking full bottles of vodka everyday and dumping the empty bottles in the morning out back.

After dumping the trash I was about to go back inside until I saw Carey's pretty face looking at mine. She was dressed in a short chocolate leather jacket and some tight jeans.

I walked up to her because something in me missed her but then I stopped short. Was she here on some murder shit? How do I know she wasn't responsible for the fire at the mansion? It wasn't like me and Ramirez didn't break her heart when we told her it was over and it was believed to have been an inside job. Maybe that was her way to get back at us.

Instead of embracing her I reached under my jacket and grabbed my gun. I slowly pulled it out and aimed in her direction. "How did you know where I lived? Huh?"

"Race, I miss—"

I cocked my gun and yelled, "How the fuck did you know where I lived, bitch?"

She froze in place. "You brought me here to make love once. You don't remember? It was right after the drama with The Russians, before Ramirez and them came back. The house was brand new at the time and everything. You didn't even have furniture."

I didn't remember before but I did remember now. I lowered my gun, tucked it behind my jeans and looked over at her. "Why are you here?"

She stepped closer and I stepped back. "I can't take it anymore, Race. I miss you too much. Can we at least talk?"

"But I told you it was over."

"I know, but you've been my everything for the past couple of years. You don't just take yourself from a person's life without a fair fight."

"There's nothing to fight about. Ramirez and me are married and we want to work on us. You not a part of that anymore."

"I understand all that but is it fair to just cut me off as if I don't matter? I know I don't have the last name Kennedy but I love you just as hard."

I looked down at the trashcan because I remembered something about my husband that I never brought up to him. He was acting distant. Although we all took the baby's death hard I couldn't justify him isolating me because of the murder.

I figured something else was up and now I would get my answers.

"You talked to Ramirez lately?"

"I told you I never reach out to him unless I have an understanding with you first. You guys broke it off with me and I miss you both. But the way to make that work is by coming to you first. So that's what I'm doing."

"Has he reached out to you?"

Her eyes moved around rapidly. "Do you really want to know?"

"Yes."

"He has called. He even showed up at my house but I wouldn't come outside. I want you. Both of you. Not just him."

Wow! Ramirez hurt me in a way I never knew was possible. He betrayed me when he didn't have to. It wasn't like we didn't bring Carey into our marriage. And it wasn't like I didn't love every minute of her being there. But I was his wife and I felt he should've told me first that he wanted her back in our lives.

And when did all this happen anyway? We just suffered a death in our family but he still found the time to reach out to another woman? The worst part about this is that she showed more loyalty to me than my own husband.

"What did he say?"

"Race, please don't do this."

I turned around to walk back in the house. If she wasn't going to answer my question I was done talking to her. I was already annoyed.

"He wanted to check on me," she said as my hand touched the cold doorknob to go back inside. "He said somebody tried to kill you all and he wanted to make sure that everybody he cared about was safe. So he reached out."

I turned around and looked at her again. "What else did he say?"

"That he missed me."

"And what did you say?"

"I said that I was fine. I asked how you were doing and if you asked about me. He told me no and that your mind was made up about the relationship being over." A tear rolled down her cheeks. " She stepped closer to me and this time I didn't move away. "Is it true?"

"Is what true?"

"Is it true that you don't think about me?"

I walked up to her and wiped her hair behind her ear. "Of course I think about you, Carey. A lot. But I made a commitment with my husband to make things work."

"But he wants me in your life. Can't you see?"

"Did he tell you that?"

"No, but I can feel it. Why else would he call and check on me?"

I was frustrated with this shit. Suddenly I didn't feel like dealing with it anymore. "Carey, right now it's not a good time. For either of us. We just lost Jasmine and it's important that we focus on the foundation. Anything else is a distraction."

She wiped some tears away. "I understand and I'm truly sorry for your loss. But you should know that I'm not walking away easily, Race. I love you too much."

"You don't love me," I responded.

"Yes I do," she said crying harder. "I loved you for a very long time."

"You don't love me, you love what I can buy for you."

She wiped her tears. "That hurts.'"

"It may have hurt but it's true. We've been taking care of you for years. How do I know that you not here because you need the money?"

"I got money. Enough to make me good for the next three years anyway."

There was a small twinge of jealousy in my stomach. Carey wasn't a working type of girl. So if she had money it was probably from another sponsor.

"Where did you get it from?"

"I started working back at the strip club. I didn't want to but I needed to make sure I was okay since ya'll cut me off. And I'm not about tapping into my savings. You know how I am," she smiled although her eyes were sad. "I'm always thinking about the future."

"Carey, I got a lot of shit on my mind right now. The last thing I need is games. If Ramirez told you that I'm not feeling the scenario anymore then what the fuck do you want?"

She sighed. "To tell you that I'm pregnant...with Ramirez's baby."

CHAPTER THIRTY

DENIM

I'm sitting on the floor of a cold tub inside of a hotel room. No water's inside of it. I drained it moments earlier to refill but I was too weak to turn the faucet back on. My heart hurt too much.

Two nights ago I left my family and the cottage like a thief in the night. I know I wasn't supposed to leave because things were dangerous but I needed to get away from everybody. I needed some rest and I couldn't do it at home. Every five minutes I had somebody opening my bedroom door and checking my pulse to see if I died yet. It got so bad that I even put Bradley out of our bedroom just so I could be alone.

I don't know what was more annoying, the fact that when my daughter first died that I wanted to take my own life and couldn't or the fact that they wouldn't let me be.

After the tub started to feel like ice on my ass I rose up a little and turned the faucet on. Immediately the warm water flowing out of the faucet comforted me. I can't believe I lost my baby. What's a mother without her child? I forgot about my life without her in it so I don't know who I am anymore.

The only thing on my mind was Jasmine and Bradley and now all that had changed.

When the phone rang I looked down at it on the bathroom floor. I turned the water off and a few splashes touched the phone's screen. It was my husband. He called me a total of 152 times since I left home even though I never picked it up.

When he stopped calling I decided to hear one of the twenty something voice messages he left. But first I had to get past all of the messages my sisters-in-law left. I just erased them until I heard Bradley's voice.

1st Message: *Baby, where are you? Why would you leave me like this? Call me.*

2nd Message: *Denim, I'm your husband and I need to know where you are!*

3rd Message: *Why are you doing this to me? You not the only one who lost a child. I'm grieving too.*

4th Message: *You won't be satisfied until a nigga goes mental. Is that what you want? Baby, please don't do this shit. I need you to call me and tell me where you are. Just tell me you're okay.*

5th Message: *In case you want to know, I'm drunk. I can't even eat because I'm losing my mind. Please come home to me, Denim. I'm dying over here.*

I knew he would be sad that I was gone but the pain in his voice made me sick to my stomach. I decided to speak to him and tell him why I left. It wasn't until that exact moment that I realized the level of pain he would experience in my absence. What was I thinking?

I was about to call him when the phone rang. I reached down and picked it up, hoping that it wouldn't fall in my bathtub.

"Bradley, I'm so sorry, baby," I said without saying hello. "I just needed to get away."

"This is not Bradley," my mother said with an attitude. "This is your fucking mother. Or have you forgotten already!"

"I'm busy," I sighed.

"Fuck you being busy. Do you have any idea what you've done to me? Any idea at all? My life is ruined and all you can do is sit selfishly in your new mansion somewhere and not answer the phone. What about me? What about your sister? We lost someone too."

I looked at the phone and put it back to my ear. The rage I felt from losing my only child was multiplied the moment I heard my mother's irritating voice. But now she took it to a whole 'nother level. She was actually coming at me like I did something wrong. Or better yet, like she had a right to come to me about anything in the first place. All she ever did was ignore Jasmine when she was around her. She never loved her!

"Ma, what are you talking about?" I asked calmly although I was breathing heavily.

"I'm talking about the fact that you left my baby in that house and she burned to death. You got out safely! Why didn't you take her? I'm talking about the fact that it is because of you that I no longer have a grandchild. I'm talking about the pain I feel right now. You are as selfish as they come, Denim Kennedy. Plain old selfish!"

I gripped the phone so tightly I could hear the screen begin to crack.

"Listen you miserable old bitch! I have done everything for you! Everything you've ever asked of me. I have washed your body when you were too fat to do it yourself. I paid your mortgage when you were too lazy to get a job. I gave you money when the men you fucked didn't care enough to give you a penny, and through it all you treated me like shit. You can't even give me the common courtesy to be there for me when I lost *my* only child."

"I'm hurting too—"

"I'm not done, bitch," I yelled louder.

My heavy breaths made me feel as if I were about to pass out. But I was so angry that I had to get everything I wanted to say out of my system first.

"Hear me and hear me good. You are dead to me. And if I ever see you or Grainger again you better pray to God I don't pull my gun on you."

CHAPTER THIRTY ONE

BRADLEY

Bradley took a moment to sit in his car before he got out and knocked on Grainger's door. He needed God's strength to deal with what he was about to do.

Although he made his money in the streets, Bradley was a God fearing man. He always knew he would have to pay for his crimes against humanity since he sold drugs and he thought he'd paid his fee when God saw fit to take his baby girl. But now he was having to deal with the loss of his wife too. Bradley Kennedy was strong but he couldn't see God putting him through that much pain. Not in one year. It would be too much.

He gripped the steering wheel inside of his car and closed his eyes.

"God, I know you don't recognize me. Why should you? I haven't done anything deserving of your love or your attention. But I'm begging you to bring me back my wife. I can't make it without her, God. If you bring her back safely I will be willing to give you anything I have, including my life."

When he was done his head rose and he looked out ahead of him. He took the keys from his car, got out and locked it with the alarm. He walked up the block leading to Sarah's house. He walked up to the door and knocked firmly. The first person he saw made him want to throw up.

A smile covered Grainger's face and she placed one hand on her hip while she held open the door. "Bradley?"

He didn't smile. Instead he got straight to the point of his visit. "Is my wife here?"

Grainger's smile was removed. "No hello or nothing huh?"

"I'm not here for all that. I'm here for Mrs. Bradley Kennedy. Is she here or not?"

Grainger opened the door wider. "Come inside."

Bradley took that as a yes and stepped into the house. It was much cleaner than it was the last time he'd been there. Just being back in the place, which almost caused him his freedom, had him wanting to kill Grainger all over again. To that day he didn't know what made Grainger change her mind about not testifying against him in court but he was silently grateful. He had a feeling it was all Denim and he wanted to repay the favor by being there in her time of need. But where was she?

"Have a seat," Grainger said sauntering in front of him. He remained standing. "Where's my wife?"

"If you're going to be rude you can get the fuck out of my house," she informed him. "Now have a fucking seat before I throw your pitiful ass out."

Bradley flopped down and looked up at her. "Where's Denim?"

She sat next to him. "She's with my mother but she'll be back soon." She looked at the clock on the wall. "About fifteen minutes to be exact."

"*Are you sure? 'Cause I'm not playing no fucking games with you.*"

"*I'm not playing no games with you either, Bradley. You aren't my problem anymore. You're my sister's. What I got to lie for?*"

Bradley held his head down. He felt like half of a man. Just a shell of himself. He wanted his family back so badly he could taste it. So he was reduced to sitting in the home of the one person on planet Earth that he couldn't stand.

"*Are you hungry?*"

He hadn't eaten since Denim went missing. "*No, I'm fine.*"

"*Do you want anything to drink?*"

His jaw twitched. He couldn't stand that bitch. "*No. I'm fine.*"

She got up and walked into the bedroom. When she returned she came back with a silver trey, a full bag of weed and some cigar paper. She sat next to him on the sofa and created a fat blunt. When it was complete she grabbed a match, lit it and inhaled. She held it in her lungs for a moment before releasing a pillow of white smoke over her head.

Bradley didn't want food or drink but he could've used a pull to release some of his troubles. Him and Denim stayed getting high. It was their pastime. So he looked over at her and wondered if she would be generous with her smoke like she was with offering him food and drink. But Grainger didn't offer him any. Instead she eyed him and finished the entire blunt by herself. By this time the sweet aroma of the smoke had his dick stiffening.

Again Grainger rolled another blunt. When she was done she lit it, took a pull and said, "*You want some?*" *She blew the smoke into his face.*

Instead of answering right away he looked into her eyes. He couldn't believe that at one point he was in a relationship with her. Bradley knew she couldn't be trusted but he needed a release while he waited on the return of his wife. And if he was high he believed he would be able to deal with things better.

"Yeah aight," he said snatching it out of her hand.

He took pull after pull until he was so relaxed he couldn't see straight. Shit was cool until thoughts of his baby girl entered his mind. During this time he allowed tears to roll from his eyes freely. But Grainger, always the snake, rolled another blunt to get his mind off of his family and back on her. For the moment she wanted to be his everything.

At the end of the night they smoked twelve blunts between them. Before long Bradley's' eyes were lowered and he stopped asking for Denim.

When he woke up the next morning he was laying on a bed he didn't recognize. He rolled over toward the window, which allowed the sun to beam onto his face. Although the rays were warm they were also bright and caused the headache he was experiencing to flare up. The light was so strong he actually thought every horrible thing that happened to him was a dream. His daughter hadn't died and his wife hadn't left him. Boy was he wrong.

He was quickly brought to reality when three cops burst into the room with guns pointing at him. Grainger was in the middle of him pointing in his direction.

"That's him right there. He's the one who raped me!"

CHAPTER THIRTY TWO

SCARLETT

I had a lot on my mind. Between Denim leaving and nobody knowing where she was, and this baby crying all hours of the night, I was starting to believe that I was in over my head. Add to that the fact that Camp had checked out on this marriage leaving me to handle things alone.

"I'm sick of this shit, Camp," I yelled at my husband while I chased him around our bedroom. "You can't move around like you don't have a family anymore. This isn't fair to me or your baby."

"Scarlett, relax," he said putting his watch on. "I'm only stepping out for a few minutes. I need a break. I'm human you know."

"You not the only one needing a break. And you say that shit all the time. I'm your wife and Master is your son and we both need you here."

"You need to calm down before you wake the baby."

"The baby is not in our room. Race has him so that I could talk to you in private."

"But he's in the house. You think just cause he's a baby that he won't know what's happening between us? This spot is not as big as the other place. Now fall back before I say something I won't be able to take back." He finished putting his watch on.

"Camp, I need your help. I need your love around here. I'm trying to do right by you but now I feel that you aren't."

"Keep it real, Scarlett. What you need is to control me and I'm sick of that shit. Every time I turn around you crying about this and you crying about that. I'm a man not some fucking play toy." He grabbed his jacket. "You know what I'm starting to believe it was a bad idea to work shit out with you."

I plopped on the bed and looked over at him. "If you didn't want me, why did you take me back? I don't understand."

He turned around and looked at me. He leaned up against the dresser. "I'm not happy."

"What does that mean?"

"It means that I thought I wanted this marriage but now I'm starting to think we moved too fast. I got caught up when I saw my son and I made a decision I shouldn't have."

"What does that mean?" I yelled louder.

"It means that when this shit blows over we have to re-think what we're doing together. So that we can be better parents."

"In other words you don't want to be married to me anymore. Right?"

He didn't answer.

"Camp, I'm begging you not to do this to me. Please. I know we have our problems and I know I'm not the best wife but I can't take this anymore. The flip flopping and the game play is not good for my emotions. You can't keep messing with my heart and then think I'm going to take it. You don't do people like that you say you love."

"You see how I asked that we deal with this later? And you see how you won't let me? Now shit is taken to the next level. All I'm saying is that I need time to think things through. Give a nigga a break."

"You think Ngozi burned the house down and killed your niece don't you? You blame me?"

"I didn't say that."

He may have said he didn't say that but I saw it in his eyes. He blamed me for everything as usual.

"I hate you so much," I yelled.

"Fuck out of here with that temper tantrum shit," he responded. "I'm not feeling it anymore."

He turned around toward the dresser. The moment his eyes were off me I ran up to him. It was like I was drawn to him like a magnet. With my fist clenched I beat him in the middle of his back and head. Because I wasn't seeing blood I moved to the sides of his face. My mission was to tear into the flesh of his skin.

I could tell he was trying to defend himself by holding my arms but he wasn't as quick as me. I'd done this before and I always won.

And that's when he did it. He did something he'd never done before. He struck me so hard in the face I dropped down. For some reason I loved it. Because it meant he still cared.

"I told you not to put your hands on me again, bitch, but you didn't listen," he said looking down at me.

"Fuck you," I yelled with hot tears rolling down my face. "I fucking hate you!"

"I don't give a fuck, I hate you too, slut," he screamed. "And it's over!"

"My brother was right. I should've never married a nig-ger."

The moment the words flew out of my mouth I wanted to take them back. I thought about my baby. My black son. I thought about the look in Camp's eyes as the words left my mouth. It's amazing how much you love someone and how deep you can reach when you're trying to cause them pain.

I never looked at Camp like he was a nigger. I never focused on our color differences even though it was obvious. But here I was going for the lowest blow I could find.

He backed away from me and sat on the edge of the bed. He placed his forearms on his thighs and looked out ahead of him. Not at me or anything in particular, he was just staring. Whenever he did this it wasn't good.

"In a month, when everything here blows over I'm going to leave," he said. "And get a place of my own."

I remained silent while he continued to destroy my world.

"And when I find a place I'm going to file for divorce." He looked down at me.

I crawled by his feet and grabbed a hold of his ankles. "Camp, please don't do this to me. I didn't mean what I said. I didn't mean to call you a nigger but you hurt my feelings. And you do it to me all the time. I was just saying shit to make you mad."

He stood up and walked away from me. "I know, Scarlett. And I'm sorry I put my hands on you. Even though we have our problems I should've never stooped so low. But you should know that I'm going to be a good father to my son, and he'll never want for anything as long as I'm alive. But we through."

"But why, Camp! Give me one good reason! I know it's something else. I can tell by looking into your eyes."

He focused on me with a lot of intensity. "Because I'm in love with another woman," he responded.

I released his legs. Now I understood. "I fell in love with her before we left for LA," he continued. "I met her when you and I were fighting."

My mouth hung because I didn't see this coming.

"She helped me and my brothers get away because she knew some people in LA and our bond became tighter. She was the one who reported to us that it was cool to come back. When we got back home I tried to deny my feelings for her because you and I were still married. I wanted so badly to work on my family and just seeing you with Master and how you took care of him made me love you and want to work things out. But I realize that although I love you I'm not *in love* with you anymore. I'm sorry."

As if he didn't just ruin my heart he grabbed his wallet and his keys. "I'm coming back in the morning." He walked out of the room.

My world will never be the same. It's one thing for us to be together and have problems, but it's a different story if a woman is involved. I feel like I can't compete. Is she black? Is she white? Is she prettier? Is she younger or older?

Slowly I pulled myself up. I went to the bathroom and washed the tears off of my face along with the makeup I wore just for him. When I was done I slid out of the pink nightgown. I slipped into a baby blue velour sweat suit and my Ugg boots. When I dressed, I grabbed my purse and went into the other room to get Master who was fast asleep.

I walked outside, put him in his car seat and drove to the gas station. I filled up the tank and drove for miles and miles. I rode in the direction of Virginia until I couldn't drive anymore. When the tank was almost empty I happened upon a set of row homes. I knew the address well.

I parked the car and walked around the back. I grabbed the car seat and closed the car door. I walked up to some steps, knocked on the door and left Master on the porch. I got back in my car and pulled off.

CHAPTER THIRTY THREE

RACE

I had a long night and all I wanted to do was rest. Earlier today I delivered the mask I had been creating for a movie production company and they loved it. They tried to give me a check for my services but I left. I told them it was a gift. That might not have been the best thing to do but it wasn't about money for me. If I don't do my art I would be done. It's my passion.

I opened the door to the cottage, locked it and threw my purse down on the table. "Ramirez", I yelled into the house. When he didn't answer I flung my keys on the table. "Bambi, Melo, Noah!"

It's funny. The rule was that nobody was to leave the house yet everybody stayed out. I'm sure security was following them though. I had one tailing me too. Denim had been gone for days and nobody knew where she went. It looks like Scarlett, Bambi and the fellas aren't home either. I guess being up in this cottage for weeks on end was wearing on all of us. I know it did on me. I was starting to get sick of my family. I was starting to get sick of everybody.

It didn't help that Carey told me she was pregnant by my husband. I was so embarrassed that I didn't tell anybody, not even Bambi and the girls. Although Carey said she wanted the abortion I've seen shit like this happen before. What was to stop her from keeping the baby and extorting us for money? This shit was all too confusing. I didn't tell Ramirez about it because I wanted time to sort things through. Plus there was another reason. A much deeper one.

Six months after Ramirez and I were married we decided to ditch the condoms and stop using birth control. We made a decision to have a baby and to try real hard. There was nothing more in the world I wanted then to be a mother so there were a few things I decided to do right away.

The first thing I did was stop drinking. At that time Bambi wasn't allowed to have alcohol so there wasn't any in the house anyway. The next thing I started doing was fucking Ramirez everyday. Outside of Bambi and Kevin nobody else was fucking more than Ramirez and me. We were loud and all over the house and I loved our lives during those times.

While we were trying to conceive I did my best to relax and to take it easy. But a year later after fucking him everyday we still hadn't conceived. I saw the look of frustration in his eyes when I failed him. He never said it out of his mouth but I knew he looked at me like less than a woman and it never set well with me.

Which was why when we went to the strip club one day and saw Carey dancing on the pole I felt like she was the answer to my prayers. She was fun, attractive and interested in both of us. When we met Carey it was the first time we didn't think about having a baby. So we traded our baby hopes with excitement by inviting Carey into our bed.

To this day I don't think if Carey didn't come into our lives that we would still be married.

When I made it to my bedroom I didn't open the door right away when I heard two voices. I took the gun out of the back of my pants and placed my ear against the door. The cool wood pressed against my ear as I heard soft giggling.

Confused I opened the door and walked inside of my room. And there she was, Carey, sitting on the edge of my bed giggling with Ramirez.

"Hey," she smiled as she reached her hand out to me. "Come over here. We were just talking about you."

My eyes rolled from her to Ramirez. "What is she doing here?" I asked him sternly.

He grinned. "What's wrong, Race?"

"What the fuck is she doing here?" I said more angrily as I stepped further into my room.

"She said she talked to you and—"

I raised my gun and shot her in the head. Her flesh splattered against the red comforter on the bed and the black lamp on the nightstand. The smoke from the barrel floated over my head and drifted away, leaving a smell of gunpowder in the air.

Ramirez's eyes widened as he looked at me and then back at her. The bitch was dead.

I killed her for two reasons. First I couldn't deal with this situation anymore. It was too confusing. Did I love her? Did I love him? Did I want her to myself? Did I want my marriage to work? Only God knew the answer so I sent her to him.

The second reason I killed her was to see where Ram's heart lied. Did he love me or did he love both of us in the same way? I needed to know. And as he sat on the bed holding her limp body in his arms I had my answer. He cared about both of us equally and that would never do for me. I needed to always be first.

Ramirez and I sat on the naked mattress. The sheets and the comforter had all been burned out back in our yard. Carey's body rested under the dirt inside of the ground along with the baby she was carrying in her body. And Ramirez would never know that she was pregnant with his love child.

It's a good thing nobody was home. Because they would've been involved in a problem that Ramirez and I caused. We needed to deal with her dead body alone. She was our property and our responsibility.

As we sat in the room, looking at the walls, we hadn't said a word to one another. I think we both were holding out to see who would speak first and I knew it wouldn't be me.

"Why did you do that?" he asked looking over at me. "Why, baby?"

"Do what?" I responded staring at the hardwood floor as if I had no idea of what he was talking about.

I couldn't look directly into his eyes. But from my peripheral vision I could tell he was crying and that made me hate him even more. He looked pitiful and just the sight of him dried my pussy up.

"So you're going to play games now?" he asked.

"She was an object but she didn't know it," I said calmly. "You shouldn't be so upset, Ramirez. Another one can be purchased for much cheaper."

"Fuck is that supposed to mean?"

I turned my head to look at him. I could tell he was distraught and I found him weak in that moment. Where was the husband who was supposed to care for me? Where was the man who up to this moment had always been so strong? Where was he?

"It means that we made a mistake. She was never supposed to be loved yet you fell hard for her."

"And you didn't?" he yelled.

"You don't know me anymore do you? You came back into my life and you can't see that I've changed. I don't view love the way I use to, Ramirez. I'm about facts, guns and money and Carey compromised everything I believed. She had to go."

"I don't know what the fuck you talking about."

"Then here me clearly now. I want a divorce."

His eyebrows rose. "So now you want a divorce?" He asked angrily. "After what we just went through together? So you saying you don't love me no more?"

"I just killed the one person in the world you loved and you never once asked me how I felt. So tell me this. Why would I want to stay your wife?"

CHAPTER THIRTY FOUR

BAMBI

I'm sitting on a plastic red chair next to Race in the waiting area at a Maryland jail. When Race showed up, the bottom of her butter colored Timberlands were covered in brown dirt. And I'd been around gunpowder enough to smell it's slight scent even after it's been hours since a trigger was pulled. She had just killed.

When I asked her what happened she said she did what she had to and since I'm covered in secrets I respected her privacy for the moment.

"I'm here for you," I told her. "If you got the saw I'll bring the knife and we'll get it done."

"I know," she winked at me.

As we sat down in the waiting area I kept looking at the entrance. I was hoping Scarlett would come because I left her a message on her voicemail. Race said she heard Scarlett and Camp fighting a few nights back so I think they're having problems too. I don't know what the fuck is going on with my family these days. Everything is falling apart.

When the Kennedy name was finally called Race and I stood up. I had no idea why Bradley was in jail but I was going to find out. We followed the guard to the back of the jail and toward a glass window. We sat down and I picked up the phone and two minutes later Bradley appeared in an orange jumpsuit.

He picked up the phone and took a seat. Although he was still handsome, he looked bad. Small bags rested under his eyes and it seemed as if he hadn't slept in days.

"Hey," he said looking between Race and me. "Thanks for coming."

I gripped the phone tightly. Since I hadn't seen Denim I was hoping that this dude didn't tell me he killed my sister. If he did he was better off right where he was.

"What's going on, Bradley?" I asked him. "Why you in here?"

"Have you found my wife?"

"What the fuck are you doing in jail?" Race said even though she didn't have a phone. She was probably nervous too.

I looked at Bradley and waited on his answer. I wanted to know the same thing. The last time I saw Bradley or Denim was when Denim walked into the family meeting wanting revenge on whoever killed Jasmine. We were in the cottage. The next thing I knew she fainted and was taken to her bedroom. In the middle of the night a few days later she left and we all tried to figure out where she went.

Bradley was blowing up her phone but Denim wouldn't answer. He told Kevin that he was going to find her and nobody heard from him. A few days later I get a call from the jail and he's here.

"I went to Sarah's house to find out if my wife was there," he started by gripping the phone tighter. "I hadn't seen her and I needed to know where she was. It was driving me crazy!" His voice grew louder. "And you know we can't get the cops involved so it was up to me."

"But Sarah's house?" Race asked.

"I know," he responded looking down. "It was stupid but I had no other choice. Grainger invited me in, and the next thing I know the cops are at the house and she's crying rape."

"Hold up, something not adding up," I said suspiciously. "How you go from sitting in the house to being arrested for rape?"

He looked down at the table again. It was as if he were trying to get his answers from there. "We were smoking weed."

Race shook her head. Denim and Bradley were suckers for their smoke and it looked like he fell into the ultimate trap. Trading his problems for getting high. But who am I to talk? I'm a drunk.

"And what else?" I said. He was leaving something out and I needed him to give it to me raw.

"And I fell asleep. She kept saying Denim was on her way back every time and I knew something was off. But every time I tried to leave she would pick up the phone and say she's on her way. I was tired."

"This shit is crazy," Race said.

"You don't know how I am when it comes to my wife. I'm not one of them type niggas who marries and not keep the vow. I promised to honor and protect her and since our baby girl died, I...I"— he took the phone from his ear and slammed it on the glass partition several times. "I can't cope!"

"Kennedy," the C.O. yelled behind him. "One more outburst like that and your visit is over."

Bradley looked back at him but didn't respond. He turned around toward us again.

"If you were smoking weed and went to sleep then nothing happened," Race said. "A rape charge can't possibly stick."

Although Race was seeing the picture in one way I knew something else was up.

"You not thinking straight, Race. She already had me on the assault charge. If she presses this rape shit they may believe her. It'll look like I'm obsessed with this bitch or something."

"Did you fuck her or not?" I asked straight up.

Silence.

"Bradley, did you fuck Grainger or not?" I asked him again when he didn't answer my question quick enough. I was growing angrier.

He sat back in his seat. "I don't know. I can't remember."

I looked over at Race and back at him. "Fuck you mean you don't know? Either you stuck your dick inside of her or you didn't. It ain't a whole lot to it, Bradley."

"I think she put something in the weed she gave me. It's either that or the fact that I was exhausted and she took advantage of me."

"She might have taken advantage but to rape her they must have your semen," Race said.

"Like I said I don't know what happened. I never had a reaction to weed like that before. Add to that the fact that I hadn't eaten or slept since Denim was gone and I don't know, maybe I…"

"I never thought you would be involved in no shit like this," I said to him. I wanted to hurt him so badly. "I knew Kevin was capable of some shit like this, but not you, Bradley. You were the good one."

"Bambi, it's not even—"

"I don't want to hear that shit. All you Kennedy niggas are the same. Think just cause you got money and a dick you can buy and get whoever you want."

"I don't know what type shit my brothers be on but I have always loved my wife and I have always hated her sister. Always. And had I not been fucked up in the head I wouldn't be in the position I am now. My only crime was falling victim to that snake's games. But the last thing I was doing was thinking about fucking Grainger. Why would I want to fuck her? For what? She's the nastiest bitch I know."

"What do you want with us, Bradley?" Race asked.

He looked back at the C.O. and whispered. "You know what I want. You're a Kennedy and it ain't a whole lot that needs to be said after that. Just make it happen." He slammed the phone down and walked away.

CHAPTER THIRTY FIVE

GRAINGER

Grainger strolled into her house carrying two bags of groceries while humming. Life for her was sweet these days. How could it not be? She managed to stop using heroin in exchange for the methadone at the clinic down the street. Her sister was probably dead on the side of the road and Bradley was locked up and in jail. Christmas had come early to hear her tell it.

She walked the bags into the kitchen, unloaded all of them and then strolled out with not a care in the world. When she bent the corner she almost fell out when she saw Bambi and Race standing up looking at her. They'd been there the entire time but she didn't notice.

"Sit down, Grainger," Bambi said calmly.

Race pulled out her weapon and pointed it at Grainger's head.

"We come in peace," Bambi continued. "For now anyway."

Grainger sat in the recliner across from Bambi. The first thing both Bambi and Race noticed was the bruise on her upper lip. Bambi took a seat on the sofa.

"What the fuck do ya'll want?" Grainger barked. *"Why ya'll all up in my house and shit looking spooky? My sister ain't here."*

"Do you know where Denim is?" Bambi questioned.

She shook her head quickly. *"No, I don't. I didn't even know she was missing before a few days ago. When Bradley came over."*

"Why are you so set on ruining your sisters' life?" Bambi asked seriously. *"Why you gotta go fucking with a bitch's husband?"*

"I didn't fuck with him. He fucked me. First he broke my jaw and then he raped me in my own house. I don't know what Bradley told ya'll but it sounds like he was lying if he said I stepped to him any other way."

"Are you crazy?" Bambi asked. *"Do you really expect somebody to believe that he raped your bum ass? Look at you. You a washed up heroin addict."*

"I was a washed up heroin addict. I've been clean for a few weeks now. And to answer your question you don't have to believe me. I know what happened and now the police do too. This time the nigga gonna pay though and no money can change that."

"What exactly did you tell them happened?"

"If I tell ya'll you gonna let me live?" she looked up at Race and then back at Bambi.

"What happened?" Bambi repeated.

What Really Happened

Bradley and Grainger were on their fifth blunt. Although Bradley was angry with Grainger he was also filled with confusion and rage about not knowing what was going on with his wife. *Sure she lost a child but he did too. His mind was going into overdrive. One puff he would be relaxed and the next he would be angry again. He couldn't get a steady moment of peace.*

"What you over there thinking about?" Grainger asked smiling at Bradley who was sitting on the couch. "Your eyes little as shit."

"I'm thinking about my wife," his neck felt so heavy it fell into the back of the sofa. He had no idea Grainger laced the blunt with meth to confuse his mind.

"You should keep your thoughts on me," Grainger said as she stroked his hair backwards. "It's better that way." She paused. "Damn, I can't believe how good you look. Even now."

"Fuck are you doing?" he asked.

"Making you feel good." She kissed his lips. "I miss you so much, Bradley. I mean can't you see what you do to me? You can't be that crazy."

"I need you to get the fuck up off of me." Although he was serious, because he was high, his voice didn't hold the hateful tone he was known for when she was in the room.

Grainger got up and looked down at him. Then she smacked him in the face. "Stupid, ass nigga. I fucking hate you." She smacked him again. "Do you hear me, I fucking hate you. You come up in my house all the time with my sister when you know how much I cared about you. We had our fights but I know you loved me. Why you break my heart like that, Bradley? It's because of you I started using heroin. I couldn't take the pain. I couldn't take seeing you with my sister." She hit him again.

With each slap Bradley felt alive. The pain on his skin mixed with the anger in his heart and the drugs in his body caused his dick to stiffen.

Grainger represented everything he despised. He didn't know what made him attracted to her to begin with. She couldn't hold a candle to Denim's beauty. But for the moment he wanted something to ease his pain and she was it.

So he pulled her down onto his lap. He pushed her skirt up and ripped her panties off. Excited, and worried he was about to change his mind Grainger tried to assist him with his zipper to free his dick but he smacked the shit out of her, causing her lip to bust open and spray blood.

Finally Bradley released his dick and he pressed into her body. For the first time in years Grainger was filled with Bradley's thickness and she was in ecstasy. There had been so many nights she prayed for the moment but she never saw how it was possible.

Bradley, angry he was fucking his wife's sister, bit the top of her breast, leaving teeth marks along her skin. Then he bit her shoulder also causing her flesh to break and bleed. He fucked her hard and rough and nothing about it was romantic but Grainger loved every minute of it.

It didn't take her long to cum and he followed behind her a minute later as he released his sperm into her body. When he was done he immediately felt bad.

She got off of him and repositioned her clothes. She went in to kiss him and he said, "Don't put your lips anywhere near my face, slut!"

She frowned. "So we make love and now I can't kiss you?"

"I didn't make love to you. I fucked you. There's a difference. And if you ever tell my wife I will kill you."

Bambi and Race eyed Grainger suspiciously after she told the story. Of course Grainger left out the part that she was a willing participant. Instead she said he raped her to make her look better.

Although she had the bruise on her lip, which was consistent with the story she just gave, Bambi still didn't believe her.

"Raise your shirt," Bambi ordered.

"For what?" Grainger frowned.

"Raise the shirt or I'll blow it off," Race said with the gun pressed to her nipple.

Grainger quickly raised the pink sweater she was wearing. Just as she said in her story there was a bite mark above her breast and her shoulder. "You see, I didn't lie." She pulled her shirt down and looked at Bambi and then Race. "Now will you guys leave me alone?"

Bambi lowered her head. She wanted so badly to believe Bradley and just like Kevin, he had let her down.

Race on the other hand remembered something Denim said after Scarlett had her baby. "You know, Bambi, Denim once told me that she wouldn't have a problem putting flowers on Grainger's early grave."

Bambi slowly raised her head. At first she looked at Grainger and then she looked at Race.

"Then honor her wishes and kill her."

CHAPTER THIRTY SIX

DENIM

I sat in the car and looked over at the cottage. I had been gone for two weeks and I needed every day of my retreat. Since I didn't have my cell phone anymore because I threw it in the toilet after speaking to my mother, I didn't know what was happening at home. To be honest I didn't want to know what was happening. I had to get away to save my own life and I would do it again if I had to. Now the only thing I had to do was get my family to understand why I left. I'm sure that would be easier said than done.

It was time to face my life so I took a deep breath and got out of the car. When I walked inside the house I immediately felt tension. Not only that, everybody was wearing t-shirts with Master's face on the front.

Bambi was on the sofa rubbing Scarlett's arm. Since she was wearing her fatigue pants, which wasn't a good sign, I knew something major happened.

Race was sitting on the floor with her back against the wall. Kevin and Ramirez were pacing the floor and Camp was sitting at the dining room table crying. I never heard him cry before. But there was one thing they all had in common, they all looked distraught.

I walked inside and locked the door. "What's up?"

"Where the fuck have you been?" Bambi asked with venom in her voice.

I tossed my purse on the floor by the door. "I know I was wrong but I had to get away. There was so much happening with me. I couldn't cope with losing Jasmine and I needed a break." I looked at Scarlett's face again. Her skin was beat red. "But why is everybody wearing t-shirts with Master's face on the front?"

"Everything is fucked up," Bambi said angrily. She stood up and approached me. "So where do you want me to start first?"

"Don't come at me all hard, Bambi. I know it was wrong how I left out of here but like I said I just lost my baby. And the way I grieve might not be the way you would've done it but it's how I handled it. Okay? Now what the fuck is going on? Or have I been cut out of the family business all together?"

Bambi backed away and sat next to Scarlett. "Ngozi got Master."

I almost stumbled backwards when I heard the news. Although I lost my baby and it would be hard to be around Master because his presence reminded me of her, I never wanted anything like this to happen.

I covered my mouth. "Oh, my God. I'm so sorry, Scarlett."

"He had Scarlett too for a minute," Camp said, "but Scarlett was able to get away. But we think"— Camp choked up— "we think he killed Master."

"Don't say that shit," Race said compassionately. "All we know is that Ngozi doesn't live at his address anymore. If we find him we may be able to find the baby."

Bambi looked like she had her own ideas but I didn't ask her about them at the moment. I would talk to her later. She always saw what other people didn't. I guess that's why she was good in the military.

Instead I lowered my head. I was away in my own world never knowing that my family needed me. How selfish! I left without any regard for my family or my husband. And then something dawned on me.

"Wait, where's Bradley?" Nobody answered me. I stood up and walked over to Bambi. "Where is my husband?"

"He's in jail, Denim," Kevin said. "Them pigs finally got him."

My eyes widened and my heart rate increased. "In jail for what?"

"For something he didn't do," he responded.

When I looked at Race and then Bambi they looked as if they knew more. "What do you mean? I'm...I'm confused."

"When you left to clear your mind, Bradley went looking for you," Bambi started. "He didn't know where to find you. The man was a mess and he ended up going to Sarah's house. And...your sister...she...I mean..."

Bambi was never at a loss for words. She said what was on her mind and she let other people sort it out. So why was she at a loss for words now?

"What the fuck happened?" I yelled.

"Grainger said he raped her," Ramirez added. "My brother's in jail because that bitch said he raped her."

"What? That's impossible...give me the phone. I'm going to call her and get this shit straightened out right now!"

"Grainger, is missing too," Race said with her hands stuffed in her pockets. "They think she's on a drug binge. Your mother been losing her mind though. You might wanna call her."

What happened to my life? I have let what was left of my world crumble. Bradley was a good man and I don't know what kind of shit Grainger was trying to pull but I know for a fact that he wouldn't touch her with a dog's dick.

I don't care what I have to do; I was going to pull my family together. That was on my life.

CHAPTER THIRTY SEVEN

SCARLETT

I was sitting in a busy train station. People with their own lives passed me by and I wondered where they were going and what they were thinking. My feet moved rapidly under me as I waited. Waited for the person I scheduled a meeting with to come.

About an hour after I'd first arrived Ngozi walked in wearing a black button down shirt with black slacks, and a chocolate leather coat. He was with his mother and I wondered why she came. We were supposed to be alone. Those were my specific orders.

They both approached the bench where I sat. His mother, Abebi, sat on my left and Ngozi took the right.

I looked over at Ngozi and asked, "What is she doing here? I told you this meeting was private."

"What do you want, Scarlett?" he asked me calmly while ignoring my question. "The last time I spoke to you, you gave me a heads up and said that your family was after me and that I had to move."

"And I put you up in a house too," I said. "And from what I can remember its way better than the place you were living before you met me. Be grateful because you got your wish."

"That may be true but I told you not to contact me unless you have the information I need. Do you have it or not?"

"I tried but I really can't," I said turning around to face him. "Too much is going on and I don't even know where it is. Bambi keeps all of that stuff away from us. For our own protection."

"Are you saying you can't because you didn't try? Or are you saying you can't because you don't want to?"

I couldn't answer his question. All I knew was that I wanted him out of town. If he stuck around and they found him and asked him where Master was he would say he didn't know. And right now Camp and I were trying to make it work because we were trying to find our baby. Getting rid of Master worked for my marriage and it actually brought us closer.

My plan was almost good but I had to make sure Ngozi wasn't found and that he didn't know that I framed him for taking Master.

"I'm saying I can't because I tried and it was too difficult, Ngozi. Just leave town, please."

I reached down between my legs and grabbed the black leather duffle on the floor. I looked back at Abedi and then at him. I threw the heavy bag in his lap.

"What is this?" he asked.

"One million dollars. Every dollar I own."

His eyes widened. "Wow. And it isn't even my birthday." He scrutinized his surroundings for a second and then looked into the bag really quickly. He closed it up.

"You have more than enough money to start all over."

"Why the urgency?" He brushed is knuckles along the side of my face. "I thought we were getting along so well."

"I'm serious, Ngozi," I said frustrated with his lack of urgency. "I need you to leave and never come back to the DMV area again. Now I might not be able to give you the information you want from Bambi, but that's a lot of money to walk away from."

He closed the bag. "And what if I don't leave?"

"Then my family will have you executed."

"They have to find me first," he said confidently.

"They will find you, and they will kill you." I touched the bag in his lap. "Take the money and leave while you still can."

Instead of answering me he smiled. I was about to give him a piece of my mind until his mother touched my face from behind me and left something wet on my cheek. She said a few words in her African tongue and laughed.

I jumped up and wiped my face off with the back of my hand. I looked over at her. "What the fuck is wrong with you?"

She smiled. "Nothing my dear," she said calmly. "But I can't say the same for you. You will experience pain like you've never imagined," she said to me. "And when it is all said and done you will die."

I looked over at Ngozi and he smiled. He threw the bag over his shoulder. "Goodbye, Scarlett. I will be in contact."

Both of them walked away, leaving me alone.

After the day I had all I wanted to do was go in the house and go to sleep. Besides I had to rethink my entire life and what would happen if my secret got out. Something told me that Ngozi was not going to go away so maybe I would have to do something I never wanted. Leave the Kennedys.

When I walked into the bedroom Camp was sitting on the edge of the bed. "We have to talk," he said seriously.

I put my purse down on the dresser. "Okay." I leaned up against it. "What's up?" I placed a few strands of my red hair behind my ear.

He looked over at me. His eyes were as pink as they'd been since he first learned that Master was gone. "Where is my son?"

My heart pounded in my chest. "I don't know, baby. Remember we went over Ngozi's house, the place he kidnapped us, only to learn that he moved?"

"I know what we did. I know we tried to find him and I know you're saying you escaped but couldn't get my son, but I'll never forget what you said to me, a few days before you had the baby. Do you remember that day? Because I do."

My eyebrows rose. "When?"

"You made me breakfast and I knocked a plate of eggs to the floor."

I remembered now. "What did I say?"

"You said, '*If you don't give a fuck about this baby, there are always things I can do to correct the situation. Don't test me, Camp. Like I said you never got the chance to really know me. But I do know you and your weaknesses.*'" He paused. "Now what did you mean by that statement?"

I felt faint. "I don't know what I meant by that. I was angry because you didn't want me anymore and there's nothing more in life I want then to be a Kennedy."

"And you were also mad that I didn't want you days before the baby went missing. How do I know you aren't lying? Did you sell my son? Did you kill him?"

"What? Of course not!"

"Who are you, Scarlett? I mean who are you *really*? How come I haven't met your parents? Why haven't I been able to find out anything from your past? Why are you more scared of the cops then we are, which is why we couldn't call on them to help find Master? Who the fuck are you?"

I walked toward him and dropped to his knees. I looked up at him. "All you need to know is that I'm your wife. I'm the one you chose to be by your side and that will never change." I coughed a little. Suddenly I was feeling ill and I didn't know why.

"Everything changes, Scarlett. Everything. Look at our lives."

CHAPTER THIRTY EIGHT
BAMBI

We are standing over Bunny's gravesite. I'm with Kevin, Melo and Noah. Kevin came to this site at least once a week. Normally he would go with the boys or by himself. But this time he wanted me to go along. I think he was trying to figure me out, and get a reaction from me. He wanted to see if I had anything to do with her death. Didn't he know that I was the master of disguises?

Kevin walked up to Bunny's huge headstone. He and the boys placed a bushel of flowers down on the grave. The cold air blew a few petals away.

"I miss you, Bunny," Kevin said. "I know I tell you all the time but I really want you to know how much me and the boys love you. Even with you being gone, there isn't a day that goes by that I don't think about you."

My stomach grumbled. I hate that bitch, even in death.

"And I'm going to get the person who took you away from me. That's a promise." He looked over at me. "Do you want to say anything to aunt Bunny?"

"Naw," I said shaking my head.

"Why not?"

"Baby, I'm just here as support for you. Nothing more. Nothing less."

"Say something, mama," Noah said with a sly expression on his face. He knew that Bunny implicated me in a letter for her death but he never told his father. "It's only right."

"Leave ma alone, Noah," Melo said looking over at me. "Everybody grieves in their own way."

"You right about that, son," Kevin said to Melo before giving me one last look. "You right about that."

What was up with Kevin? Did he know something after all? And if so who told him?

I'm in Cloud's bedroom riding his dick as he sits on an office chair. I decided to hook him up before he told Kevin about Bunny, especially after today. Every time he touches me…every time he looks at me, I'm disgusted. I can't believe I got myself into this situation.

I have so much on my mind right now. I wanted to know if Scarlett finally went too far and killed Master. I wanted to know if Bradley would get off for the rape of Grainger. I wanted to know if Denim was handling the loss of her baby well or was she breaking down more inside. More than anything, I wondered if Kevin knew I was involved with his beloved aunt's death.

Since Cloud knows that I killed Bunny he does everything he can to make my life a living hell. Like fucking me three times a week, making me cook meals for him, which I always laced with piss. Worse than all was when he forced me to say I loved him.

I was having sex with him for one hour and he still didn't cum. Cloud thinks I'm stupid. I know for a fact he can come quicker than this. I tried to buck my hips wider and each time I did he would tell me to slow down so he could make it last. I was losing my patience with this nigga.

"Cloud, I gotta go," I said in a seductive tone.

I hate this punk.

"Can you hurry up, baby?" I continued. "You know I want to hook you up but I got things to do at home."

He ran his hand up my back and it made my skin crawl. "Slow down, Bambi, I just want to enjoy you for a minute longer. I know you in a hurry but I got you for the moment."

I stopped moving my body. I looked down at him. "You do know we not together right? This is a business relationship."

"I know," he frowned.

"Then why you keep taking your time and shit?" I asked with rage. Fuck being nice. "I can't be here all night. I'm a married woman."

"I know you married," he said with an attitude. "But I also know you not the wife you cut out to be. So stop faking in here like you are."

Fuck this nigga! I'm better than this. So I stood up and walked toward the bed to grab my panties. I felt him looking over at me, stiff wet dick and all but I didn't care.

"Where you going?" he asked.

I slipped into my jeans. "Home. Like I said."

"But I didn't bust yet."

"You acted like you didn't want to." I sat on the edge of the bed and grabbed my grey Ugg boots on the floor. "So I got shit to do. I'll look out for you next time though. Don't trip."

He stood up and walked toward me. He pulled is pants up and rubbed my shoulders. He squeezed hard but I didn't stop getting dressed.

"You are beautiful, Bambi Kennedy." He exhaled. "Why didn't you ever want me? I mean what was it about Kevin that you liked so much?"

I put one of my boots on. "Don't be stupid, Cloud. Kevin met me first. Kevin loved me hard and he always had my back. Unlike some people I know."

"But the nigga cheated on you."

"And you knew about it. That may be true but when I asked you to keep it real you didn't." I looked up at him. "What you didn't know was before that moment you could've been mine because I was always soft on you. But you failed the test."

"I can't let you leave right now. You know that." He pulled his dick out and rubbed it on my bottom lip. "Suck the cum out of it and you're free to go."

He's so gross!

"Whatever we were doing I'm done," I told him. "I have a lot of shit going on at my house and in my life right now. I can't be—"

Cloud slapped me so hard I fell off the bed and dropped to the floor. My chin landed on my other boot. I hopped up preparing to fight this nigga until the season changed to summer.

"Do it, bitch," he dared me. "Put your hands on me and I will end everything in your life. You know how much that nigga loved his aunt. Do you really want to know life without being a Kennedy? I can ruin your world. You know that!"

He grabbed me by the hair and pulled me up to him. He licked the rest of the blood off of the corner of my mouth and smiled.

I looked into his eyes. I could tell he was serious. The way I saw it I had one option. So I pushed away from him and walked over to my purse. I grabbed my cell phone out of it and dialed a number.

"What are you doing?" he asked with wide eyes.

I didn't respond. My heart beat rapidly as I waited for my call to be answered. When it finally did I took a deep breath. "Kevin," I said staring into Cloud's eyes. "I'm over your cousin house. Meet me over here. We have to talk."

Kevin was standing up while I sat on the couch with my hands over my face. Cloud was leaned up against the wall quietly.

"Baby, are you going to tell me what's going on?" Kevin asked me. "You got me on edge now and I don't like how it feels."

I looked up at him. "It's about Bunny."

"What about her?" he sat next to me. I couldn't speak or look at him. "Bambi"— he placed his hand softly on my knee— "talk to me."

I looked over at Cloud and a tear rolled down my face. I couldn't believe I was being placed in this position but I was done with the pressure Cloud was putting me under. I was done letting him play in my body. I was done trying to keep him from snitching on me. I was done with it all.

"I killed her."

Kevin smiled like a kid at first. As if he didn't understand what I was saying. "Baby, what you talking about? It sounds like you are telling me that you killed my auntie."

I wiped the water from my face. "That is what I said. I killed Bunny."

He hopped up and moved away from me as if I was dog shit. He paced the area in front of me and then stuffed his hands in his jean pockets. "What...do...you...mean?"

I stood up and moved toward him. "Kevin, I know this is fucked up but-"

"I'm sure it was a reason she did it, man," Cloud said in an attempt to come to my defense. "Just hear her out."

Although Cloud thought he was on my side I didn't want his help. I didn't want any more reasons to be at his mercy.

"I don't need your fucking help," I yelled at him. "Stay the fuck away from me! Do you hear me? Stay the fuck away from me and my family."

Cloud looked angry but he backed down and leaned against the wall again.

I focused back on Kevin, "Baby, you know me. You know I would never do anything like that unless I felt I didn't have a choice. She was blackmailing me. When we thought you were dead she tried to extort all of the money you left for the boys and me. I needed that Russian deal to go through or I wouldn't be able to take care of my family. Of our family. So I took her life. It was the only way."

He looked at me hard. His nostrils flared and his fist balled up. I could tell he hated me but couldn't find the words to express himself. There wasn't any need though. I could feel how he felt about me even in silence.

"I could kill you right now," he finally said.

I know I was wrong but I hated how hard he was coming at me. As if he wasn't wrong in this scenario too. "I guess you would want to kill me considering you were fucking your own aunt the entire time."

His expression turned from hate to guilt. "I don't know what you talking about."

"Yes you do, Kevin! Kill the fucking games! She told me everything before she died. She wanted me to know that although I wore the ring, that she was the main woman in your life."

"She lied."

I didn't respond. He and I both knew the truth. He took two steps closer to me. He squeezed my chin softly and raised my head so that our eyes met. "The day my boys turn twenty-one," he said sweetly, "you're going to pay for this. With your life." He walked around me and toward the door.

My back remained in Kevin's direction and then I remembered something. Before he left out I took the gun out of my waist. "But what about—"

"Kill him," he said referring to his cousin. "I knew you were fucking him from jump and I didn't know why. Now I do." He walked out and slammed the door.

"Kevin, noooo," Cloud yelled before I raised my gun and put a bullet in the middle of his head.

The moment his body slumped to the floor I had an orgasm. A real orgasm. You have to understand that I hated that mothafucka! With a passion. He ruined my life and it felt good to get the revenge I deserved. I was about to tuck my gun back in my waist when my phone rang.

As if I didn't just kill a nigga, I walked over toward my bag and grabbed my cell. I placed it to my ear, looked over at his corpse and said, "Hello."

"Bambi, shit is getting even crazier around here," Race said to me.

"How you figure?"

It wasn't like Master wasn't missing, Jasmine wasn't dead, we didn't kill Grainger and Bradley wasn't in jail. How much crazier could things get?

"Scarlett has a high ass fever. Should I take her to a hospital?"

"No," I said shaking my head. I'm glad she called me before doing anything stupid. With The Russians still being silent we needed to stay low. The last thing I needed was one of my family members hanging around a hospital, out in the open. The last time we went to the hospital I was shot in the hand. "How high is her temperature?"

"It's in the one hundreds but that's not even the worst part."

"Then tell me what is."

"She said she got the fever because...well... because...well you gotta come home and hear this shit."

I made it to my house an hour after I burned Cloud's house to the ground. It wasn't hard for me to come up with the fire idea. Someone had done the same thing to the Kennedy compound. Since they got away with it maybe I could too.

I threw my purse on the couch and ran toward Scarlett's room. Race was hanging around her as if she were on her last breath. Scarlett's eyes were closed and she was moaning softly.

"What were you trying to tell me on the phone?" I asked placing the back of my hand on Scarlett's clammy face.

"This shit is so crazy," Race said. "She told me that somebody put a curse on her and she was about to die."

"A curse?" I frowned. "What do you mean?"

"She actually said voodoo but I don't know what happened. All I know is she could barely get out of bed when I came in the room to check on her. I'm worried. This don't look too good."

I looked down at my sister. "Scarlett and that voodoo shit. She probably fucked up because Master is missing. This girl been through a lot lately. Where the fuck is Camp and everybody else?"

"Camp took a bag of clothes and left. I think they broke up. And Ramirez went to see Bradley in jail. Where's Kevin?"

Some where with his heart broken. I thought.

"He probably not coming home until later either." I looked over at Race. "He knows I killed Bunny."

She covered her mouth. "Bambi, no."

"I know but I had to tell the nigga. I couldn't deal with Cloud's blackmailing ass no more. And I put Cloud out of his misery too."

"Are you okay?"

"I'm a soldier," I said honestly. "Of course I'm okay."

Race focused back on Scarlett's weak body. "You sure we shouldn't take her to the hospital?" she asked me with a serious look on her face. "I've never seen anything like this."

"No, you know she on paper. We just gotta break her fever." I threw the covers back on the bed. "Go run a tub full of ice cold water. When I was in the army we did this type of shit all the time."

Race ran to the bathroom while I peeled the nightgown off of Scarlett's damp body. Her face was flush red and my heart broke. I loved this chick like we came out the same pussy. And with everything that happened in my life lately I couldn't lose her.

I don't know what's going on but I do know this. If you believe somebody put a curse on you, with all your mind and body, your body will grant your wish. The mind was stronger than most people gave it credit. Add to that the fact that Scarlett's weird aunt practiced voodoo. This girl didn't have a chance. But I believe that there's another reason she's so sick. Guilt is killing her. The guilt of what is the real question.

I took her temperature before doing anything. It was 107. When Race was finished running the water we hoisted Scarlett's naked body into the tub. Scarlett mumbled a few words but for the most part she moaned softly. Her pink nipples hardened and stuck straight out in the air as she sat in the water. I didn't know I would be seeing a white girl's body in my lifetime. I guess I was wrong.

When we were done we dried her off, put some clean warm pajamas on her body and placed her back in bed. I stayed over her for an hour, pressing cold rags over her face while Race gave her sips of ice water.

"I feel terrible," Scarlett finally said as I placed the thermometer on her tongue.

"Close your mouth," I said softly. When it beeped I read the temperature. It was 105. I placed it on the table beside her. "Scarlett, what's going on with you? Why you sick?"

"I'm going to die," she said as a tear came down her face. "I'm going to die because of all of the things I've done wrong in life."

"Don't say that," Race said. "You not a bad person. You're a—"

"Yes I am," Scarlett interrupted. "I'm a horrible person and now a curse has been placed on me and I'm going to die." She looked over at me. "But I don't want to."

"Scarlett, you can't believe in no shit like that," I told her. "I don't know why you're sick but it's definitely not because of a curse. It's deeper. Much deeper."

"Ngozi is killing me."

I wanted more information but she drifted off to sleep. I hopped off of the bed and went through her bedroom.

"What you looking for?" Race asked me.

"I gotta get this nigga's information."

"Who?"

"Ngozi."

"But he moved remember? We went looking for him to find Master."

"I believe Scarlett knows more about his whereabouts than she's letting on. You heard her. Ngozi put a curse on her. That means she hooked up with him recently."

After fifteen more minutes I found Scarlett's phone. I tried to get into it but the screen was locked. "Fuck," I yelled in frustration. "I don't know the code."

"Good luck getting it from Scarlett," Race said with her arms folded over her chest. "I remember I wanted to use her phone one day when she left it at home because Melo was on the house phone on school business and my phone had 2% battery power left. I used my weak phone to call Scarlett who was with Camp at the time. To ask if I could borrow her phone. I asked her what the code was to unlock it and everything."

"What happened?"

"Nothing. She wouldn't give it to me. My phone ended up dying and I had to wait until Melo finished with his class project."

"She's going to give me that code," I said.

I walked over to Scarlett's bedside again. I sat on the edge of the bed. Real softly I said, "Scarlett, what's the code to your phone?"

She moaned a little but she didn't respond. I touched her on the arm. "Scarlett, I need the code to your phone. If you want me to help you you gotta help me. Now what is the code?"

She moaned a little and said, "I don't feel good." Her eyes remained shut the entire time. It was as if she were dreaming.

"I know, but I need the code to your cell phone." When she stopped talking I gently shook her. "Scarlett...the code. What is it?"

When I looked over at Race she was wearing the *I Told You So Face.*

Frustrated I stood up and paced the floor. I needed the code so that I could go through her phone and bring this nigga here. I figured if she saw him and he took back whatever fake crazy hex he put on her that things would be okay. But since she wouldn't respond to me I couldn't help her.

Suddenly Scarlett moaned and said, "9267."

I turned around to look at her. Her eyes were shut. I was about to ask her to repeat it but I wanted to try it first. So I placed the numbers into the phone and it unlocked

I looked at Race and winked. "I'm in!"

CHAPTER THIRTY NINE
BAMBI

I was sitting outside of Ngozi's house in a black Suburban. Sarge was in the driver's seat and three of my men were in the back. Sarge and Race handled any murder jobs I had within the Pretty Kings Empire. I met him when I was in the military and we'd been good friends ever since. Whatever I needed Sarge to do he did. There was one problem, he was also atrracted to me.

I found out two weeks ago when we had to break the teeth of every nigga running the Dunbar Projects in Washington DC. The leader, Enny, had been short for two weeks straight when it came time to picking up the profits. When Race and Sarge went to question him and his crew, each member blamed the other. It was totally unorganized. So I had Race and Sarge order our soldiers to handle the problem. It wasn't a dry face on the block that day because each one was covered in blood.

Later that night, Sarge reported to me what happened at the Kennedy Compound. It was just he and I because Kevin wasn't home. Me and Kevin got into a fight over his baby mother and I was crying, something I preferred not to do especially around other people.

Sarge gave me a hug and told me everything would be okay. I realized at that moment how much I truly cared about him. He got me out of binds when we were in the service together and he was like a father to me. But when he leaned in and tried to kiss me I knew he looked at me differently. I told him if he promised to never make a move on me like that again that I would forget it. But if he did it again, he would be cut out of my operation and my life forever. He never did.

After sitting at the house for what felt like forever, Ngozi and some older woman pulled up in a silver BMW. We stooped down a little in the trucks to prevent from being seen.

"That's him," I said to Sarge. "I'd know that face anywhere."

We waited for them to get out of the car and go into the house. When they were inside I sat up straight and said, "Let's go get that nigga."

All of us crept toward the house like we were in the field in Saudia Arabia. I realized I was in my element. War would always have a part of my heart, which is probably why I always found myself submerged in drama.

When we got up to the house Sarge moved toward me. "How do you want to get in?" he asked.

I crept toward the front door and kicked it in. "Like this!"

My men flooded the house and me and Sarge approached Ngozi and the older woman who were standing in the living room. They appeared caught off guard.

The other soldiers went through the house to make sure the coast was clear. Sarge's gun was aimed at Ngozi and the woman and I stood in silence as we stared at one another.

"What are you doing here?" Ngozi asked me.

My head tilted and I stared at him. Where was his African accent? The one Scarlett loved so much because she said it gave him international appeal.

"The house is clear," one of my men said as he and the others stood behind Ngozi and the woman. They were armed and ready.

"Who are you?" I asked Ngozi.

He cleared his throat and suddenly his accent returned. "I'm Ngozi. I—"

I smacked him with the butt of my gun and his tooth flew out of his mouth and spun on the hardwood floor like a spinning top.

"Who are you?" I repeated.

He stared down at the floor. Bloody mouth and all. He resembled a kid who's hand had been caught digging into the cookie jar. Except his hand was about to be chopped off instead of slapped.

"My name is Nathan Avenues."

I moved closer toward him and my soldiers tightened in on both of them. "I don't give a fuck about your name. I want to know who you are."

He looked at the floor. "I'm, I'm working for—"

"The Russians," I said shaking my head.

I felt so fucking stupid. How did I not see this coming? It makes so much sense now. This dude came into the picture right about the time Kevin and our men came back. The Russians must've hired him to get the connect information they wanted from me.

"I'm sorry," he said, "I didn't."

I put my hand out to shut him up. "What's going on with Scarlett? Even if it was about the money, why would you tell her you put a hex on her? I'm not understanding."

"We got carried away," the older woman said in a Boston accent. "She told Nathan, or Ngozi, that she was afraid of the occult. Me and Nathan have been married for five years and when he told me what The Russians wanted I thought of a way to get it. So I brought to life what she was already scared of."

I felt my pressure boiling over. "Where's Master?"

Nathan looked at his wife. "Master? Who's that?"

"The baby? Where is the fucking baby? Don't play games with me."

"On my life I don't know what you're talking about."

I figured he wasn't involved. Scarlett had some questions to answer.

"Did you burn down my house?"

"No," he said under his breath. "But I'm not going to lie, I did use it to my advantage when she approached me. I figured if she thought I was capable of something like that she would give me what I wanted. The Russians threatened to kill me and my wife. I was afraid."

"But their was accelerant all over the house. Only somebody with access to our home could've done that."

"It wasn't me. That's all I can tell you. I did give her the voodoo doll but that was the extent of it. I swear on my life!"

I don't know why but something told me he was telling the truth.

I looked over at Sarge. In my heart I knew he didn't have anything to do with the baby going missing or the fire but I couldn't tell Scarlett. Right now there was one thing on my mind, taking him back to the house. I figured if Scarlett heard this dude speaking in perfect English that she would know he was a fake. But that was only the beginning of my plan.

CHAPTER FORTY

BAMBI

Ngozi and the older woman were on the floor in Scarlett's room bound and gagged. Sarge and my other soldiers hung around them in case they made a move. Race stood against the wall and I carefully walked over to Scarlett's bed and sat down on the edge of it.

"Scarlett," I said softly. "I need you to wake up."

She moaned a little and said, "What's going on?"

"Open your eyes and wake up." I paused. "I have something for you. Somebody I want you to see."

She slowly opened her eyes and looked into mine. "What is it?"

"Ngozi is here."

She looked horrified and moved toward the edge of the bed as if he was about to kill her. "What is he doing here? Don't let him get me! Don't let him hurt me."

"Scarlett"— I placed my hand on her arm— "he's not going to hurt you." I nodded toward the floor. "Now look at him."

Her upper body rested against the headboard. "How do you know?" she asked shivering.

"Because he's a fake. He's not from Africa or anywhere else. He's working with The Russians. They were using him to get to you."

I looked into her eyes to see how much she knew. I could tell she wasn't totally innocent. What The Russians didn't know was that I didn't leave the connect information lying around. I kept that in the safest place on earth. In my mind.

I walked over to Ngozi and kicked him. I snatched the tape off his mouth. "Tell her! Tell her the fucking truth."

Ngozi ran his tongue over his lips I guess because they were dry. "I'm sorry, Scarlett," he said. "I really am. I didn't know things would go so far."

Race walked over to them too. Up until that moment she didn't know he didn't have an African accent or that he was gaming Scarlett. I didn't have a chance to explain anything to her when we first got here because time was of the essence.

"Wait, this nigga not from Africa?" Race asked.

"No," I said in disgust. "He's from Virginia, Alexandria to be exact. Not too far from the Woodrow Wilson Bridge."

Scarlett sat up in bed. She was still flushed but already she was looking better.

"So she didn't put a curse on me?" Scarlett asked looking at his wife.

"Why ya'll not talking?" I asked looking down at the wife. "Tell her what type of shit ya'll on."

"I'm his wife, Scarlett," she said in a shaky voice. "And I didn't put anything on you. I don't even know voodoo. I knew you were afraid so I decided to play a little with your mind. It was all a game but I wasn't trying to hurt anybody."

"What did you put on my face at the train station?"

"Spit," she said with a stupid smile.

I didn't know what they were talking about but I knew it was making Scarlett feel better. I could tell.

"Well if they didn't do anything to me, why am I sick?" she asked me as if I were a doctor.

"Because you making yourself sick. Maybe you got something on your heart that you have to get off. Only you know the real answer to that."

"Fuck all that. Where's the baby?" Race asked Ngozi.

I raised my gun and shot Nathan before he gave an answer. And then I shot his wife. Their blood drained out of their bodies and into our carpet.

"Why you do that shit?" Race yelled angrily. "We don't know where Master is!"

I don't know why I chose to protect the fact that Scarlett lied on him about kidnapping the baby but I did. I made a decision to find out from her later where Master was and I didn't want Race involved. Not right now anyway. Besides, she had her own problems to deal with.

"I killed him because he doesn't know anything," I said to her. "I asked him when I picked him up from the house."

I sat on the edge of Scarlett's bed. "I need you to get yourself together. And I need you to do it quickly too. You can't let somebody get in your head like that again. It's dangerous to you. It's dangerous to your family and it's dangerous to our operation. Am I clear, Scarlett? Because there can be no more mistakes."

She leaned back in bed and gave me *the thank you for keeping my secret* look.

"We're clear," she said smiling. She touched my hand. "And thank you."

As I looked over at her I realized there was still some unanswered questions. For instance if Ngozi didn't burn the house down, who did?

CHAPTER FORTY ONE
THE DAY THE HOUSE BURNT DOWN

Jasmine was in her room playing with one of her dolls on the floor. She was combing the doll's hair and decided that she wanted to make her face as pretty as her mother's but she didn't have any makeup. But she was smart enough to know where some was.

So Jasmine took her doll and walked downstairs to the basement to aunt Race's studio where she kept all of the pretty makeup and scary props.

Ramirez warned Race about locking the door but with everything going on in her life, Race didn't remember. And because of it a child was able to get into the dangerous area.

When she made it downstairs, Jasmine placed the doll on the silver worktable and grabbed a small can of red paint from one of the counters. She'd seen her aunt Race use it on many occasions when she would sneak in her studio unnoticed.

Jasmine twisted the cap off of the paint, grabbed a paintbrush and painted the dolls lips red. But it was sloppy and not as nice as the work she'd seen Race do so she wanted her mother's help.

Jasmine grabbed the cylinder of paint remover she also saw Race use and her doll. She walked up the steps to get her mother. Jasmine didn't realize that the paint remover was open and leaving a trail from the basement to her parent's bedroom.

Jasmine placed the cylinder down along with her doll by the door and knocked hard.

"Who is it?" Denim yelled while she and Bradley made love in the bedroom.

Jasmine was scared and didn't know how to answer so she remained silent. She could tell her mother was frustrated. Denim, thinking someone was playing grew irritated.

"Who the fuck is it?" Denim yelled louder. "I'm not playing!"

"Mommy," Jasmine said softly. "Can you help me?"

Denim didn't hear her daughter ask for help but she did hear her say mommy. But Denim was making love to her husband and didn't want to be disturbed. With the case over Bradley's head for breaking Grainger's jaw, she wanted to spend some alone time with him because she didn't know how much longer he would be free.

"Wait a minute, Jasmine," Denim yelled. "Come back later!"

Disappointed, Jasmine grabbed her doll and the cylinder and went to the kitchen downstairs, spilling the paint remover the entire way. She placed the doll and the cylinder on the counter.

She was going to pour herself some orange juice but when she opened a drawer she saw some matches in a tiny red box.

Jasmine had seen her mother fire up blunts when she thought Jasmine was sleep so she knew how to light matches. She opened the small box, removed a stick and struck it against the side of the box. Her eyes brightened when she saw the spectacular orange flame before her.

Fascinated she blew it out and did it five more times. But the sixth time the match fell out of her hand and dropped to the floor, directly into the paint remover.

The fire immediately caught onto the carpet and then the kitchen towels. Afraid, Jasmine grabbed her doll and hid in the bathroom, some feet over from the kitchen.

Because the paint remover was everywhere, it only took seconds for the house to be engulfed in flames. And since aunt Bunny removed the batteries from the fire detector before she was murdered, to enact a future plan to kill Bambi, the detectors didn't work and the fire ignited.

Little Jasmine was burned alive in the bathroom.

CHAPTER FORTY TWO

BAMBI

When I walked into our kitchen, Scarlett was sitting at the table eating the homemade chicken soup I made earlier. The house was pretty quiet. So much had happened since we killed Ngozi.

Race was looking for a house of her own and told me she filed for divorce. Camp and Scarlett banned together to find their son and Kevin and I barely spoke anymore. Denim was always at the jail visiting Bradley and when she wasn't there she was over her mother's house trying to calm her down because Grainger was still missing. My twins were in college with round the clock security even though they didn't want it.

Even though everybody was doing their own thing it was virtually impossible to get a day like this because somebody was always coming and going in the cottage. But today was different. It was just Scarlett and me.

"Hey, Bambi," Scarlett said before sipping some hot soup from a huge yellow cup. "It's quiet around here right? How you feeling?"

I walked over to the counter and grabbed a white soup bowl. Then I walked to the stove and scooped out some soup. I carefully walked to the table and sat down. I tasted the soup. It was just right.

"I'm fine."

She looked over at me. "You don't look like it."

I smiled. "When are you going to tell me what really happened to Master?"

She sat the soup cup down. "I don't know what happened to him," she said under her breath. "We're trying to find him. I hope it's soon too."

I just stared at her. I wanted her to know that I could see right through her. She placed a thick strand of hair behind her ear.

"What, Bambi? Why you looking at me like that?"

"Where's the baby?" I asked firmly. "Is he alive or not?"

She stared ahead of her and a tear rolled down her face. "You always knew me. When everyone else saw around me, you always knew the truth. Why?"

"Because I care. Now is he alive?"

"Yes."

I looked down into my soup at a piece of celery that floated around in the bowl. "Why would you get rid of him like that? This doesn't make any sense, Scarlett."

She sighed. "I have a few reasons. But it was mainly because I couldn't take care of the baby anymore, Bambi. I'm dangerous with a child. I don't trust myself. You know that. I figured this way the baby would have a chance at a real life."

"But we would've helped you. Your sisters and me. You would not have cared for him alone. You had three other women willing to pick up the slack."

She smirked. "How? I mean let's be realistic, Bambi. You got your hands full with Melo and Noah and don't get me started on whatever you got popping off with Kevin. Even if you couldn't help me let's suppose I tried to rely on Denim. Who by the way likes me every other day and then hates me the rest of the week. She's focused on Bradley and the fact that her sister is missing. The only person who's left is Race. And when am I going to get a hold of her? She stays in the streets checking on the operation and when she's not she's out trying to buy a new house. There's no way that you or anybody else would've been able to help me with Master. I would've been all alone. Now imagine a sick mind alone with a helpless baby. I know my limits, Bambi. Trust me. So I had to give him away to protect his life."

I put my head down because she was right. "I wish you would've come to me. We could've figured something out better. Instead you got everybody wearing 'Find Master' t-shirts when you no he's never coming home. God forbid Camp ever finds out what you did with his son."

"Well, I guess we all got secrets huh?"

"Not me. Kevin knows what happened to his aunt now. I'm secret free."

"For now," she said sipping more soup. "But you and I both know that you collect new secrets everyday."

"Where did you leave him?"

"With a family I found when I first discovered I was pregnant. Before Camp came back." She sighed. "They are a God fearing family and they will love Master very much. That's why there were no reports of the baby being found in the news. He's safe with them. I'll give you the address so you can check on him from time to time yourself. Just don't knock on the door or let them see you." She paused and in a lower voice said, "I've driven by the house a lot. Trust me, he has a much better mother than I could ever be."

"I hope what you're doing is right."

"It has to be," she replied. "But look, I don't wanna talk about that anymore. What's going on with The Russians?"

"I thought about them a lot. They couldn't get what they wanted from me or you so what happens next?"

She looked up at the ceiling as if she was trying to figure it out. "I don't know," She shrugged.

"Well I do. So pack a bag. We're taking a trip."

EPILOGUE

The sun was beaming in Monetary Mexico as Mitch McKenzie; the Kennedy Kings' connect blasted Caribbean music in his brick mansion. When his doorbell rang he grabbed the remote control and pressed a button. The music was reduced instantly. He waited for his wife to answer it but she must've been in the garden behind their home.

Mitch walked to the door and opened it. When he saw Bambi he was pleased and nervous at the same time. What was she doing at his home. To her right was Race and behind her was Scarlett and Denim. The sun stood behind them and bounced off of their bodies. Turning their shapes into sexy silhouettes. They all were wearing tight jeans with bikini tops. Bambi's was camouflage.

"Bambi," he smiled weakly. "What's going on?" he looked at the other Pretty Kings. "Why didn't you tell me you were coming?"

"I'm sorry but maybe you'll forgive me. Besides we come baring gifts," Bambi said. "Something we're sure you're going to like."

Bambi turned around and two Mexican locals brought in a beautiful wooden table. They sat it in the middle of the floor. Bambi tipped the men.

"Gracias," one of the men said.

"De nada."

After Bambi tipped the two men and they exited Mitch said, *"Where are my manners?"* he opened the door wider. *"Come inside, ladies."*

He was trying to be pleasant, to imply that he had control over the moment. But truthfully he had no idea what was happening and he felt helpless, which was so unlike him.

Bambi sat on the recliner and Mitch took a seat on the couch in front of her. The other Pretty Kings remained standing behind Bambi.

Mitch looked over at the handcrafted table that resembled a box. It was the most beautiful thing he'd ever seen.

"Where did you find it?" he asked trying to conduct small talk.

"It's custom-made. Just for you."

He swallowed. *"But what are you doing here?"*

Very calmly she said, *"I'm here to save your life."* She crossed her legs. *"And you can thank me later."*

He stood up and walked toward the bar. He poured himself a glass of whiskey. *"I'm done with the hospitality. You have my address but it doesn't mean you have an open invitation to come here any time you'd like. Now be clearer! I'm a very busy man."* he swallowed all of the whiskey and slammed the glass down on the bar. *"What are you doing here?"* He poured himself another drink.

"I'll get to that. Let me first give you the status of your affairs here in beautiful Mexico. I had your armed guards held up at the gate leading into your property. I guess they aren't use to things happening to you so they didn't see us coming. Don't worry though. We're much smarter than they are."

He appeared embarrassed at the lack of professionalism of his soldiers. *"I'm a very busy man, Bambi."* He turned *around and faced them. "And I want the point of your visit now."*

Bambi stood up and moved toward him. When she was in his breathing space she eased the drink out of his hand and took a sip. "I never took you as rude." She drank the rest of it. "As much money as I made you and you didn't even offer me a drink." She winked. "We have reason to believe that The Russians are in Mexico right now looking for you."

"And?"

"And unless you want you and your family to be bound, gagged and raped, like their track record has proven, you're coming with me. Today. Right now."

His eyes widened. "Linda," he said calling out into the house for his wife. "Linda, where are you?"

"She's not here," Bambi said calmly. "She's already away to safety."

Mitch was beyond angry. When he was dealing with the Kennedy Kings he never had this problem. He was the connect and nobody ever found out about his whereabouts. And now there he was trying to defend himself.

"We have to move now," Race said looking out of the window. "They are about fifteen minutes from your house."

"And unfortunately we can't let anyone see you leave," Bambi added.

"And how do you plan on getting me out of here safely?"

Bambi turned around and looked at Denim who opened the lid on the table. "You're getting inside of there. Now."